FALCON'S FOX

Sandrine Gasq-Dion

Sandrine Gasq-Dion

Dedication:

First and foremost, Kody Boye and Bradley Mathis.
Thank you, for your strength and openness.
My wonderful editor, Jenjo.
Ann Lister
Brenda Cothern
As always, Aarin, Doug, and James.
Brandon and Tyler of The Green Room
City of Flagstaff
The Tihan Network

Author acknowledges the following trademarks:
Spaceballs; Metro-Goldwyn-Mayer Studios, Inc.
FIAT: FIAT-Group Marketing Corporate
Communication
Guinness: GUINNESS®
EEGEE's, INC
Wicked Arizona Coffee L L C
Starbucks®

Sandrine Gasq-Dion

Author's Note

This book was a long time coming. I had to pick the right couple and tell the story the way I knew it needed telling. I want to thank all the people who made this book so easy to write. The characters' love for one another through good times and bad inspired me.
It's not about gay or straight.
It's about LOVE.

The Players:
Ransom Fox
Gareth Wolf
Jinx Jett
Harley Payne
Rebel Stryker
Paul Vincent
Grandpa Stryker
Sal Falco
Sebastian Lowery

Sandrine Gasq-Dion

The Bodyguards:
Axel Blaze
Achilles Castellanos
Hammer aka Marcello Balboni
Buster aka Kirk Kendrick
The Boss, Mac Collins

The Band Manager:
Stan Jackson

The London Boys:
Jayden Dempsey
Evander Torrin
The Spiros Twins, Dimos & Dimas

FRET brings Gareth and Axel Blaze together
JINXED brings Jinx and Jayden together
HARLEY'S ACHILLES brings Harley and Achilles together

Table of Contents

Sandrine Gasq-Dion

Prologue

3 months earlier, at Sebastian Lowery's Hollywood Hills home.

I should have brought Scarlett with me. What was I doing here alone? When Sebastian called and invited me to his house for some Hollywood party, I should have said no. Scarlett had begged off tonight due to a headache. I couldn't really blame her. She attended every single premiere with me as my girlfriend, so taking the night off from a party was fine by me. I entered Sebastian's house and looked around for the man of the hour. As I scanned the room, my eyes caught sight of the man about whom I'd been dreaming for years.

Ransom Fox stood across from me in all his delicious glory.

"Sal!" Sebastian strode up to me and I leaned into his ear.

"Please tell me you're going to introduce me," I said quietly.

"I sure am," Sebastian chuckled.

I'd known Sebastian since we were in our teens. He'd

come to America to make it big and I was on a sitcom that my dad was producing. Sebastian had tried out for a role and lost it, but we got along great and I introduced him to my father. That, as they say, was that. Sebastian had begun acting in films and eventually turned to producing. Sebastian curled his fingers around my bicep and walked me across the room. Ransom looked petrified to meet me, it seemed. He had a wild, panicked look in his eyes.

"Ah, Ransom Fox. I would like to introduce you to my dear friend, Sal Falco." Sebastian pushed me closer to Ransom and he appeared to stiffen.

"What a pleasure, Ransom. I love your music," I began smoothly.

"Wait, what?" Ransom stammered.

Sebastian introduced me to Jinx Jett, the band's drummer, and I shook his hand, but my attention focused solely on the gorgeous blond in front of me. Jesus, could God have made a more perfect specimen? Ransom Fox was a wet dream.

"Can I offer you a drink, Ransom?" I motioned to the bar.

"Oh, um, I don't really drink much." Ransom bit his bottom lip.

Oh, fuck me. Damn, he was sexy when he did that.

"Water, maybe?" I smiled.

Jinx coughed and pointed to the corner. "I'll just be

10

over there."

"Uh huh." Ransom nodded, his eyes fixed on me.

I held my hand out, indicating we should move toward the bar, and Ransom started walking. I fell into step with him and pulled out one of the high-backed chairs. Ransom jumped onto it and I took the one beside him.

"So, you, um, like my music?" Ransom fiddled with a napkin, his attention focused on the wooden top of the bar.

"I really do," I admitted. "I've been into metal since I was a kid."

"I loved you on that show *Neighbors*. Your character was hilarious with all the shit he got himself into."

"You watched that?" I asked in astonishment. "That was my very first show."

"The writing was fabulous. I would watch it religiously. When that ended, I watched *Park Place*. You were such a bad boy in that," Ransom laughed.

"Well, I was in my late teens, so you know they had to up the angst." I motioned to the waiter and asked for two waters. Ransom's eyes met mine and a blush colored his cheeks. "You could have been an actor with your looks, you know."

"Oh no. I get camera shy and I'm really not all that." Ransom shook his head.

Was he blind? Ransom could have given me a run for

my money as a leading man. He was drop-dead, fine-as-all-fuck.

"You don't give yourself enough credit, Ransom. I'm sure you have women all over you."

"Because I'm a rock star," Ransom pointed out. "None of them would want me if I wasn't who I am now."

I wanted him on the bar, naked and screaming my name. I had to stop looking at him like he was the last cannoli on the plate or I was going to give myself away.

"No one would want me if I was just plain ol' Salvatore Falco."

"Are you kidding me?" Ransom's eyes went wide. "Have you seen —" Ransom clamped his mouth shut and sipped his water.

"Have I seen what?" I leaned in with a grin.

"Your reviews," Ransom blurted. "All the women want you."

I leaned back in the chair and eyed Ransom. He was biting at his bottom lip again and I wanted to bite it myself. He was a little shorter than me, lean but defined. His forearm held a smattering of tattoos and I wanted to lick them. I wondered if he had more, and where they were. Ransom cast a glance at me and I smiled.

"I can't stay long, but I was hoping we could continue this discussion at some point?" I asked.

"Sure." Ransom nodded.

"Well, here's my card with my cell phone and email. I hope to hear from you soon, Ransom. Maybe next time you're in town we can have dinner?"

"Oh, um, sure. I'd like that." Ransom's head bounced up and down and I couldn't help my smile. Ransom Fox was the guy I'd always wanted. Too bad I could never have him.

Chapter 1

I hated Los Angeles. I really did. You couldn't pay me to live here. I lived in Flagstaff, Arizona, where the bulk of our traffic came down historic Route Sixty-Six. And even that wasn't bad compared to this clusterfuck. I exhaled in frustration as the car in front of me moved two inches. I'd been stuck in this shit for an hour already and it wasn't looking much better up ahead. I should have taken a limo instead of driving myself in this tiny Tic-Tac of a rental car, but I just couldn't see myself rolling up to a hotel in a limo. It just wasn't my style.

My little brother and I grew up with barely any money. Our parents loved each other, but they had their nights when they fought like cats and dogs. It was on those nights when Gareth and I would disappear either to our treehouse or a little fort we'd made out of cardboard boxes. I smiled at the thought of Gareth and the tree house. It hadn't really been a house, just some plywood as far up as we could get it. Now, Gareth owned an honest-to-goodness tree house. My little brother had been through hell when our former band manager — and my best friend — Paul Vincent wanted to return to the band and take Gareth's place. Now I knew that Paul was sick, that he had PTSD and clinical depression resulting from the car accident that had taken his ability to play guitar and led to Gareth replacing him.

Gareth had gotten a husband from among the bodyguards assigned to protect him when he began to get death threats. Jinx Jett, my drummer, had found love with his little boy-bander, Jayden Dempsey; and Harley Payne, my rhythm guitarist, had fallen in love with his own bodyguard, Achilles Castellanos. That left Rebel Stryker and me without love. Well, who knew if Rebel had love? He had someone every night. I didn't think that was love. That was just sex.

Some kinky sex nonetheless. I chuckled at the thought.

My phone beeped and I looked down at it. My heart began to race as I saw Sal Falco's name on the screen. A month ago, we'd held a fundraiser for an LGBT youth center and Sal had emceed. After that, I didn't think I'd hear from him. He basically disappeared right after his duties were done. I felt like I'd done something wrong somehow. Had he figured out that I had a huge crush on him? I swiped talk and braced myself.

"Hello?"

"Hey, Ransom. I heard you're in town."

"I am. I'm moving Paul to Arizona, so I have to settle things out here."

"Well, if you're free tonight, could we have dinner?"

I swear I was sweating just from talking to him. I needed to get my shit together and act like a fucking man for fuck's sake.

"I could do that. I'm not due at the hospital until morning, anyway." I told him which hospital and the line got quiet for a second. I was just about to say something when Sal began talking again.

"Well, where are you staying? I can pick you up."

"I haven't decided yet. Whatever's closest to the hospital."

"I'm actually not that far. You could stay with me."

I choked on my spit and then broke out in a hacking fit.

"Ransom? Are you all right?"

"Yep," I coughed. "Swallowed my water wrong."

Stay with Sal? That was just begging for me to fuck up. I knew I acted like I had my shit together, but when it came to Sal Falco — I was a teenage girl.

"I'll text you my address, if that's okay? You don't

have to stay here."

"No, that's fine."

"Okay, I'll see you when you get here."

"Okay. Thanks, Sal."

I hung up before I could say something really stupid. Two seconds later, Sal texted me his address. Luckily for me, the exit I needed was right ahead.

I finally got off the freeway and headed toward Sal's house. Palm trees lined the roads and manicured lawns stood out like square-cut emeralds. Tall gates surrounded beautiful houses as I finally turned onto Sal's street. I checked my phone and slowed down, looking at house numbers. I didn't really need to, though, because Sal was standing in front of a house two down. I pulled up to the open gate and lowered my window as he approached the car.

"How do you fit in there?" Sal peeked into the car. "Does it plug in?" Sal started laughing.

"This is what happens during a holiday weekend. You get the last of the cars on the lot. It was this or a huge gas guzzler."

"Why didn't you just get a limo?"

I lifted a brow and Sal laughed again.

"Well, come on in." He moved away from the car and I followed the drive around to the front of the house. I had to admit, I didn't know what I was expecting, but Sal's house was very low-key. Palms and roses covered the entire front of the house and a small waterfall off to the side watered lavender. I got out of the car and popped the trunk. I bent in to get my bag and Sal brushed up against me. My whole body reacted and heat pooled in my balls. I righted myself quickly and pulled my bag out, closing the trunk. We walked to the front door and I took a long look around. Sal came to my side and opened the door.

"This is beautiful," I told him.

"Thanks. I like to bring a little bit of Europe to my houses."

We entered the foyer and I set my bag down on the hardwood floor. Plants sprung up in every direction I looked and there were paintings of vineyards on the walls.

"You have a gorgeous house," I complimented him.

"It's all thanks to me."

I turned to find a gorgeous redhead in jeans and a ratty T-shirt addressing me. Her makeup was flawless, but she was wearing slippers.

"Ransom, I'd like you to meet Scarlett. My girlfriend."

My gut sank at those last two words. Scarlett was breathtaking. I'd seen her before in pictures, but in person she was even more beautiful.

"It's nice to meet you." I stuck my hand out.

"Well, my, my. Ransom Fox," she purred. "You are

even more handsome in person."

"Thank you. Pictures don't do you justice, Scarlett," I responded.

"And he's polite." Scarlett lifted her brows at Sal. "Are we keeping him?"

Sal chuckled. "He's just staying here while he gets his friend's affairs in order."

"Well, if you need anything, you just call on Sal there. He'll take care of your every need." Scarlett grinned.

Sal coughed and shot her a look. I tilted my head and observed them. "Where should I take my stuff?"

"It's down that hall, last room on the right," Sal answered.

"Thank you."

"How about dinner? Still up for it?" Sal asked.

"Oh. Maybe you and Scarlett want to go out?"

"Not me, sweetie. I have lines to run. Maybe next time? I'm sure Sal wants you all to himself." Scarlett batted her eyelashes at me. "So good to meet you."

"You as well. I'll just go get settled, then?"

Sal nodded and I took off down the hall. That had to be the weirdest conversation I'd heard in a while. I dropped my bag just inside the guest room and peeked around. More pictures of vineyards and a few of Sal's movie posters covered the walls. I walked up to one of them and just stared at it. Sal was just... wow.

"Settling in?"

I jumped at the voice behind me and Sal chortled.

"Sorry," he snickered. "Hungry?"

My stomach chose that moment to growl and I smiled sheepishly. "I guess I am."

"Well, I know this great place not too far from here. They serve Irish food."

"Aren't you Italian?" I asked.

"Yes, but you're not," Sal pointed out.

"We don't have to eat Irish food just because I'm Irish."

"Maybe I like Irish food." Sal cocked a brow.

"Oh really? What's your favorite?"

"I'll find out once we get to the restaurant."

I laughed and Sal blushed. I wanted him right then. He looked so... vulnerable. Why, oh why did I have to be infatuated with a straight man? I raised my eyes to find Sal watching me and the look in his eyes caught me off guard. He coughed, straightened, and backed toward the door. "Yell when you're ready."

"Okay."

Fuck, how the hell was I supposed to keep my thoughts clean when I was going to be around this man for God knew how long? I'd wanted Sal Falco from the second I saw him on TV.

Fuck my life.

I unpacked some of my clothing and hung it in the closet. I grabbed my favorite pair of jeans and threw on a grey T-shirt. I looked down at my arms and contemplated wearing a long sleeve shirt. I had a ton of tattoos on both arms and I didn't know what kind of place we were going to. I pulled on my boots and walked back out to the foyer. The room was quiet and I peeked around the corner into the living room. A grand piano positioned near large floor-to-ceiling windows drew me over; the view of Hollywood was spectacular. I looked out at the city and pursed my lips and whistled in appreciation.

"Like it?"

I glanced over my shoulder and nearly passed out. Sal was wearing worn, faded jeans with a dark blue button-up shirt. His hair was neatly styled, closely shaved on the sides but with length on the top.

"It's beautiful, don't get me wrong —" I began.

"Yeah, I know. I've lived here all my life and I still don't know why I do."

"It's just so... pushy. Even on the road they ride your ass. Fuck, at least pull my hair and call me Daddy."

Sal busted out laughing and it enveloped the whole room. I laughed too because his laughter was just damned infectious.

"Whoa. That was good." Sal wiped at his eyes.

I composed myself and pointed to my shirt. "Is this okay to go out?"

"Yeah, we're not hitting a five-star establishment. Unless you want to?"

"Nah, I'm not good with the rich."

"You are rich," Sal pointed out.

"Yeah, but I'm not hoity-toity rich."

"Meaning?"

"I still stop to give the homeless money, I work in soup kitchens during the holidays, I give to veterans, and I spend time with them. I don't know too many richies who do that. Do you?"

"I'm starting to feel inadequate." Sal smiled at me sheepishly.

"Oh, sorry," I mumbled.

"No, it's okay. You just gave me a lot to think about. It's easy to write a check, but I should be doing more."

"I really didn't mean to insult you —" I babbled.

"You didn't," Sal interrupted me. "Like I said, you gave me a lot to think about. Are you ready to go?"

"Yes." I nodded.

Why did I have to go on like that? I probably made him feel like shit because he wasn't serving soup to the homeless. I was a ginormous asshole.

"Ransom?"

"Yeah?" I glanced up and saw Sal's huge grin.

"Stop beating yourself up. You made a valid point."

The last thing I wanted was to make Sal feel like shit. I had known this was going to happen. I couldn't say the right thing in his presence. The teenage girl was present and bopping her pigtails around.

Sal opened the garage and my mouth dropped open. Four cars sat side-by-side, all of them black and shiny. Sal walked over to the smallest one and threw me a grin.

"A Fiat? Will we both fit in there?" I chuckled.

"We will, and I don't have to plug it in."

"Ha, ha."

I climbed into the car and was surprised at the legroom. I was six feet tall and Sal was a bit taller than me. We pulled out of the garage and hit the road. Sal maneuvered between cars and down side streets and, before I knew it, we were parking in front of the place. I got out and took a look around.

"Come on in." Sal motioned to the front door.

I walked in and surveyed the surroundings. Four-leaf clovers, each with someone's name on it, covered the walls. The floor went from carpet to polished bricks and the booths were back-to-back with green upholstery. It was actually kind of homey. A large, burly man with sideburns walked out and grinned.

"Mr. Falco! So good to see you again! Would you like the same table?"

"Aye, Fergus," Sal spoke in an Irish brogue.

"You're getting it, son!"

We sat down and picked up menus. I perused mine and then peeked over at Sal. He was watching me. I swallowed hard and I was sure everyone could hear it.

"Um, you already know what you're getting?" I asked.

"Same thing I always get."

"I see you've been here before."

"Yep. I did a movie where my character was —"

"Irish. Yes, I saw it."

Sal leaned forward, propping his elbows on the table. "Have you seen all my movies?" he asked, head tilted.

"Yes," I admitted.

"Really? What was your favorite?"

"*Delta Flight*. You had one of the best lines in that movie!" I laughed.

"Your 'check asshole light is on'," we both said in unison.

"I actually ad-libbed that one," Sal admitted with a grin.

We both cracked up, and then I sobered as the waitress brought our water.

"You ready to order, boys?" she asked.

"Shepherd's pie and a Guinness, Maggie." Sal handed her back the menu.

"I'll have the pan roasted pork chop and the same, please." I handed her back the menu as well and her eyes went wide as she placed me.

"Holy shit," she whispered.

I grinned. "Nice to meet you too."

"I know I shouldn't ask, but could I please get your autograph later?"

"You can get it now," I told her.

"Thank you! Hang on, let me go get something for you to sign!"

I chuckled and glanced over at Sal. He was smiling from ear to ear.

"What?" I asked.

"You're so down to earth. I've heard it a million times from fans, but you really are laid back, aren't you?"

"I'm just plain ol' Ransom," I winked.

Sal must have remembered our conversation from a few months back because a grin split his lips and he laughed lightly. The waitress came back and I signed a menu for her. We took a picture together, courtesy of Sal. I kissed her cheek and she reddened.

"Do you want one with Sal?" I asked.

"I see him all the time." She winked and sauntered off.

I turned my attention to the man in front of me and lifted an inquisitive brow.

"Okay, so I come here a lot," he admitted. "I really do like Irish food."

"Have you ever had it in Ireland?"

"I actually have. The movie I shot was in Dublin, so I got to eat the food and drink the beer."

"I would love to go and just relax there. I mean, we get to see some stuff on tours, but it seems like I'm always working. I want to stop and appreciate everything around me."

"I know what you mean. I didn't get to sightsee in Ireland. About the only time I get rest and relaxation is in Italy, visiting my folks."

"I love Italy."

Our waitress came back and dropped off our beers and Sal excused himself to use the restroom. As she placed my drink down, I smiled up at her.

"So, he comes here a lot?" I asked.

"May I?" She gestured to Sal's empty seat.

"Of course."

Maggie sat down and smiled at me. "That man is a saint. When my daughter turned four, Sal showed up at her birthday party dressed as his animated character from *Reef Tales.*"

"Squishy the Squid?" I laughed.

"Yes. She'd seen the movie four times in the theater, but Sal brought a copy of it with him. It was her birthday gift from him. He stayed the whole day and played in the bouncy castle with four-year-olds."

I shook my head with a smile. "I had no idea."

"That's not all he's done. When Fergus' son had leukemia, Sal paid for all his medical bills." She smiled sadly. "When he passed, Sal paid for the funeral. It took a toll on him."

"What was his name?" I barely whispered.

"Patrick — or Paddy, that's what we called him. See that picture over there on the wall?" She pointed behind me and I twisted in the booth to see. "That's Paddy when he was in the hospital. Sal came to see him every day. Mr. Falco doesn't broadcast the things he does, but we all know the kind of person he is." She wiped at her eyes and stood. "I'll go check on your food."

"Thank you."

I was awed, and twisted again to see the picture of Sal with a little boy. He had a smile on his face and an arm wrapped around a child I now knew was Paddy. My eyes began to water and I blinked a few times to clear them. Sal came back to the table and eyed me curiously.

"Is everything okay?" he asked, taking his seat.

"Yes. I'm fine."

Our food arrived, stalling any conversation for a few minutes. I took a bite of my pork and sighed in bliss. I loved home cooked meals, but didn't get to make them too often.

My kitchen skills were seriously lacking. Gareth was the guy who could cook in our family.

"Good?" Sal asked.

"So good."

"So." Sal leaned back a bit in the booth and eyed me. "You're here to move your friend Paul back to Arizona."

"Yes. I came for Christmas so he wouldn't be alone, and then I went back home for a couple days. I was going to come back after the New Year, but things have changed in our group. This New Year's Eve is going to be a lot different for the guys and me. Jinx, Gareth, and Harley all have someone to share it with, and Rebel and I didn't want to encroach on their time."

"So what is Rebel going to do for the New Year?"

"Try to keep his grandpa clothed?" I laughed.

"That bad, huh?" Sal laughed.

"Rebel's gramps is in the beginning stages of Alzheimer's, so Rebel has to watch him closely. He has hired a few nurses to watch after him, but they all quit."

"Oh? Why?"

"Let's just say Rebel's grandpa is very flirtatious."

Sal cracked up and I shot him a grin. We turned our attention back to our meals. I was finally starting to feel at ease with him. He really was a nice guy. I'd seen all of his interviews and he always came across as a very generous man. Now I knew he really was. I knew his parents were both in the movie business back in the day, and that's how Sal got into the movies when he was a child.

"So you want to watch the newest movie I'm in?"

Sal interrupted my thoughts and I peered up at him. "Really? I thought it was still in production?"

"Nah, it's in the editing stages but I have a rough cut."

"Are you kidding me? Hell, yes, I want to watch it!"

Sal chuckled. "You really do like my movies, huh?"

"Duh." I pointed at him with my fork.

"Well, let's finish up and get a move on."

We finished up and were paying the check when a couple walked in and began to talk to Sal. He introduced me and then excused himself for a few minutes. I stared at all the pictures on the wall. I felt a presence at my side and glanced over to find Fergus standing next to me.

"He's a good man, that Sal."

"He really is," I agreed.

"Saved my restaurant. Maggie said she told you about Paddy. What she doesn't know is that I almost lost the place trying to pay the medical bills. I was in a bad place and refusing charity, but Sal let it leak to reporters that he ate here a lot and then BAM! There was never an empty seat in this place. I finally let him pay the bills but I told him I'd pay him back."

"Let me guess," I grinned. "He never takes your

money?"

"Tells me to give it to charity." Fergus searched my eyes. "I can see he's taking a shine to you. I don't listen to your music, but I hear you've done very well for yourself."

I nodded and then caught a look in his eye. "Oh, I have my own money, Fergus. I like Sal, and not for his money or fame."

"Good to know." Fergus winked.

Sal walked up to us, clapping Fergus on the back. "Good to see you, old friend."

"You both have a good night." Fergus shook my hand.

"Ready?" Sal asked.

"Yep."

Chapter 2

I was nervous as hell driving back to the house. Being with Ransom felt so natural, I found myself staring at him longer than I should. I already knew a lot about him. He was very open in his interviews, but I felt as if I needed to know more. I wanted to know what made him tick, what made him smile.

What made him scream.

The house was empty when we got back and I let out a slow sigh of relief. I loved Scarlett, but she knew about my infatuation with Ransom Fox. The second I saw him, I wanted him. And when I found out what kind of person he was? I was smitten instantly. I walked into the kitchen with Ransom right on my heels.

"Popcorn?" I asked.

"I think I still have room for it. Besides, what good is watching a movie without movie staples?"

"See? You get it," I laughed.

I made the popcorn and then we settled on the sectional in the living room. I threw off my shoes and sat cross-legged as I pushed play on the DVD player. Ransom did the same, reclining back on the couch, the bowl of popcorn between us. The first scene in the movie had me running down a back alley, gun poised and ready to shoot.

"Do you have a stand-in for these scenes?" Ransom asked.

"For the more dangerous scenes, yes. If I'm falling off a building or something, my stunt double does those."

"Look at you run. You're not even breathing hard." Ransom chuckled.

"Well, they did call 'cut' when I tripped."

Ransom cracked up. "So, you're obviously a cop in this, right?"

"Actually, no. I'm the youngest son of a high-powered Mafia family."

"Oooh! Interesting!"

"Yes, right now I'm chasing a rival Mafia man."

"So, what's the plot?"

"I'm tired of the old ways, I want to make things better within the organization. My family has other ideas. I'm forced to marry the youngest daughter of the rival family, but I fall in love with the wife of the rival."

"Ouch. That causes problems, I take it?"

"Well, if you watch the movie, you'll find out." I snickered.

Ransom playfully slapped my bicep and focused on the movie. I couldn't help but watch him. He had a beautiful profile. His nose was straight and rounded on the end. His bottom lip was a bit plump and he had a strong, square jawline and chin. He shaved his blond hair on the sides with length on the back and top, styled with some kind of product. He was just... perfect. The credits rolled and Ransom turned to me with a grin.

"I think you might get another Oscar for this one."

"Nah. I just did this one for fun."

"It's an awesome storyline, Sal."

"Well, I'm glad you liked it."

Ransom stretched his arms out and his T-shirt rode up, revealing smooth skin and his happy trail. I licked my lips and averted my eyes.

"Tired?" I asked.

"I actually am." Ransom checked his watch. "God, how sad am I? It's only nine."

"Jet-lagged, maybe?"

"Maybe." Ransom shrugged. "I think I'll just shower and hit the hay." Ransom stood and I stood too. He extended his hand and I shook it. "Thanks for putting me up, Sal."

"No problem. Get some sleep."

As I watched him go, half of me wanted to follow him. Who the fuck was I kidding? All of me wanted to follow him. I heard the key in the front door and Scarlett strode in with a grin.

"How was dinner?"

"I thought you were running lines?"

"Oh, I did. I went out for drinks after about two hours. So, again, I have to ask: how was dinner?"

"It was fun." I walked toward my room with Scarlett following. I closed my door after she entered and plopped down on my bed. Scarlett came to my side and touched my cheek.

"Are you sure this was a good idea to have him here? I could see the hunger in your eyes, Sal."

"This is the perfect test for me. If I can keep my hands off of him, I'm golden."

Scarlett leaned in and kissed my temple. "I want you to be happy, Sal. You've wanted Ransom Fox from the second you laid eyes on him. The world is changing. You could come out."

"I can't. God, do you realize the backlash I'll get?" I shook my head. "I can't. I won't."

"Then you are bound to suffer for the rest of your life, Sal. You're always going to be alone. You're thirty-one. You should be serious with someone, planning a family, getting married."

"I only want one man," I sighed, curling up on the bed.

"Then make a move. The worst he could do is punch you. Besides, his brother is gay. He's not homophobic in the least."

"Haven't you been paying attention? His brother, their drummer, and rhythm guitarist are with men now."

"Wow." Scarlett frowned. "Who does that leave? Sexy Rebel Stryker and Ransom."

"Sexy Rebel Stryker?" I lifted an inquisitive brow.

"Hell, yes. I love that he's tatted to shit." Scarlett chuckled. She sobered and touched my cheek. "Please, think about it, Sal. I don't want you to be alone forever."

"I'll think about it." I took her hand and kissed it.

"So, do you mind if I go visit Ransom tonight?" Scarlett wiggled her brows.

I laughed and hit her with a pillow. "Get out!"

Scarlett left, laughing as she did. I jumped in the shower and thought about the sexy lead singer on the other side of my house. Ransom Fox drove me nuts. He was everything I'd ever wanted in a man: lean, but defined, beautiful eyes which seemed to change color from green to peridot, and luscious lips.

I dried off and got into bed, rolling to my side. I stared at the clock and hoped morning would come soon.

I wanted to spend as much time with Ransom as I

could.

I was up by eight in the morning. I couldn't believe I'd slept in so long. I was always up at four and out the door by five to make it to the studio. Now that the movie was in edits, I had some downtime. I made coffee and grabbed the carton of eggs out of the fridge along with some bacon. Scarlett walked out, hair in curlers and in her sweats.

"Leaving for the studio?" I asked.

"I have a late call, so yeah. I have no idea when I'll be back."

Ransom walked out into the kitchen and I almost dropped the bacon. He was shirtless, wearing low-rise jeans and there were droplets of water cascading between his pectorals. He was running a hand through his wet hair and was carrying a shirt in his free hand. My mouth dropped open and Scarlett came to stand in front of me. She lifted my chin and made me look at her.

"Get it together, hon," she whispered.

"But…"

"I know. I'm seeing it too." Scarlett winked. "Be

good!"

"Oh, are you leaving?" Ransom asked.

"Gotta go, sweet cheeks. You take good care of Sal, 'k?"

"Um, okay." Ransom turned to me with a small grin. "Are you planning on cooking that?"

"Oh! Yeah. You like bacon?"

"Are there people who don't?" Ransom's brows furrowed.

"If there are, something is seriously wrong with them," I laughed.

I made the bacon and whipped up the eggs, making them into an omelet. Ransom pulled his shirt on and I almost sighed at him covering all that beautiful flesh. I served him a plate complete with toast and then sat across from him.

"So, you're going to the hospital today?" I asked, taking a bite.

"Yep," Ransom mumbled around his mouthful of food. "This is really good."

"Thanks. Could you use some company? I really don't know what to do with myself if I'm not working."

Ransom seemed uncomfortable and I swallowed my food and caught his eyes.

"Sorry, I shouldn't have asked."

"It's not that. Um, it's a long story, but I guess you

could come with me. I'll explain in the car."

Once we were in the car, Ransom began to fidget. I really shouldn't have invited myself along, but the thought of not seeing him for hours didn't sit well with me. This was such a bad idea. The more time I spent with Ransom, the more I liked him. Was he good looking? Hell, yes, but his personality had me from the get-go. The car was uncomfortably silent and I fought for something to say to break the ice.

"Not too many people know this, so I'd ask you to keep it to yourself," Ransom said, breaking the silence.

"Of course. You have my word."

"When Gareth first came out, he was getting a lot of death threats. I mean, really bad ones that scared the shit out of me. I talked to Paul about it and he agreed we should hire a bodyguard for Gareth. Paul contacted this really expensive security place and they sent out Axel Blaze."

"He's Gareth's husband, right?" I interrupted.

"Yes, now he is. So Axel gets Gareth to the concert here in L.A. safely and then there was an incident."

"I heard about that."

"It all came to a head while we were in Europe. As it turned out, Paul had been behind everything."

"What?"

"Yes. Gareth figured it out and they had a

confrontation at a hotel. Paul shot Axel while Axel was protecting my brother. Paul has PTSD and clinical depression. He wanted to come back to the band as lead guitarist and thought getting rid of Gareth would accomplish that."

"Oh, God. I'm so sorry, Ransom."

"There's more. I didn't know how Paul felt about me. I mean, we messed around as teenagers, but it was never serious."

"Wait — you messed around?" I turned to look at Ransom and noticed his face turning red.

"Yeah. I guess he loves me, or loved me. I don't know anymore, but he was jealous of Gareth because, since he was sick a lot, I spent most of my time with him. He almost killed my brother because of me."

"That's not your fault, Ransom."

"Why do I feel like it is, then? I didn't lead him on afterwards. I mean, we haven't been together like that since we were fifteen."

"That's not your fault, okay? Paul is sick and you got him help. I don't know if I would have been as forgiving as you."

"For a split second, I wanted him to rot in jail. Gareth and I talked about it and we agreed Paul wasn't like that before the accident. He was never cruel and he did love Gareth back then. He gave Gareth his first guitar. I knew it had to do with his illness."

"Your brother is one hell of an exceptional man, Ransom."

"Yeah." Ransom grinned. "He really is."

We pulled into the parking lot of the mental hospital and I cut the engine. I turned in the seat and eyed Ransom. He glanced over at me and I swear his eyes were changing colors right in front of me.

"I can stay in the car," I offered.

"Um, no, it's cool if you come."

Ransom got out of the car and began walking ahead of me. He stopped right outside the doors and I noticed a wall of a man standing at the entrance, arms crossed, looking as if he was ready to kill someone for looking at him.

"Buster?" Ransom began walking again. "What's up? Everything okay with Paul?"

"Yeah. Mac sent me out here to keep an eye on things."

Buster zeroed in on me and I began sweating. The guy was seriously scary.

"You mean keep an eye on me?" Ransom stopped in front of the man and placed his hands on his hips.

"You, Paul." Buster locked eyes with me. "Him."

"Me?" I almost squeaked. Almost.

"You are in Ransom's company, and you have your

own weirdos. Ransom needs to be kept safe."

"I'm a black belt." I stared him down. "I think I can watch Ransom's back."

"Really?" Ransom turned to look at me.

"Yeah," I admitted. "I do my own fight scenes."

"That is so cool," Ransom mused.

"*So* cool," Buster drawled. "But to be on the safe side, I'll be around."

"Stop being a dick, Buster." Ransom shoved the man.

"But it's my specialty." Buster mussed Ransom's hair.

"Ack! Stop it!" Ransom batted Buster's hand away.

I could see the affection the bodyguard had for Ransom. It occurred to me that I should be glad the guy was here watching out for him. It was true — I did have my own weirdos. I'd had fans break into my house before and tail me when I went out shopping.

We entered the hospital and Ransom went to the sign-in desk. I stood off to the side trying to blend into my surroundings. The bodyguard was watching me like a hawk and I finally had enough.

"What?"

"You like him," he stated baldly.

"Whoa, hold up a sec —"

"Ready?" Ransom walked up on us. He looked from me, to Buster, and then back to me. "Everything okay?"

"It's fine." I shot a look at Buster and he merely grinned.

"You coming, Buster?" Ransom asked.

"I'll be right here."

I almost sighed in relief when we walked down the hall, leaving the brooding, scary-looking wall of muscle behind. Ransom stopped in front of a door and knocked softly. He cracked the door open and I got a peek at Paul Vincent. Paul was sitting at a weight bench, pushing what appeared to be a lot of weight. The guy was seriously good looking, with jet-black hair and the darkest blue eyes I've ever seen. He was about Ransom's height and wearing a T-shirt with no sleeves. Tattoos covered his biceps and a there was a guitar tattooed on his neck.

"Paul?" Ransom pushed the door open a bit more and walked in. I followed and leaned against the wall. Paul set the barbell down and wiped the sweat from his brow. There was a brace around his right hand and his other hand sported a glove for weight lifting.

"Hey, Ransom!" Paul smiled.

The two of them hugged, and Ransom stepped back, eyeing Paul.

"You look good."

"So do you." Paul eyed Ransom from head to toe. I squirmed at the intense once-over Paul was giving Ransom. My hackles rose and Paul noticed me and shot me a knowing grin. I hated that I was so damned transparent when it came to Ransom.

"Well, well. Sal Falco! What brings you here?" Paul asked, walking over to me.

"I'm staying with him while I'm in town," Ransom answered.

"Is that right?" Paul pumped my hand, all while watching me intensely.

"I offered," I blurted stupidly.

"I bet you did." Paul winked.

Shit. Fuck and damn. Paul knew. He fucking knew.

"How's that sexy girlfriend of yours?" Paul crossed the room to get a bottle of water and I stared at Ransom.

"She's fine. Working today. I bet you're excited to be going back home, aren't you, Paul?" I asked.

"I really am. God, I hate Los Angeles." Paul sighed. "Oops, sorry. I know you call this home."

"Don't worry about it. There are days I wonder why I don't move."

Ransom cut in. "So, um, your doctor said it should only take a couple of days to get you cleared out and checked in over at the hospital in Arizona. I guess there's a lot of paperwork involved and the doctors are going over your care with each other."

"That's what he said." Paul sat down on the end of the workout bench and sipped his water. "I'll just be glad when I'm back to my old self. They changed my meds again, so I'm adjusting." Paul eyed me cautiously. "Ransom told you everything?"

"Yes, he did, but I swore I'd never breathe a word of it," I vowed.

"I trust him, Paul," Ransom interrupted. "I hope it's okay that I told him?"

"I trust you, Ransom, and if you think Sal can keep a secret, well, then, he can."

"You know I'd never do anything to hurt you." Ransom took Paul's hands in his.

"You really don't need to worry about me, Ransom. I'm doing okay. I really am. I just need to learn how to forgive myself. Gareth keeps telling me to do it, but I can't just yet."

I could see the history between them and damn if I wasn't jealous. Ransom said he didn't feel that way about Paul, but watching them together, you'd think they were a couple. It was *really* starting to bug me.

"I'm going to find your doctor, okay? I'll be right back." Ransom turned to me. "Do you mind staying here?"

"Nope. Take your time." I nodded.

Ransom left, closing the door behind him. I looked directly at Paul. He was smiling so wide I thought his lips would crack.

"Oh, you got it bad, doncha, Sal?" Paul stood and

walked toward me. "Don't hurt him, got it?

"What makes you think I like Ransom in that way?" I defended myself.

"Oh, please! Your body language when he hugged me. Everything in your stance is defensive, like you want to pounce on me and kick my ass. Trust me, what Ransom and I had was years ago and he wasn't even really into me."

"I have a girlfriend, Paul," I reminded him.

"Does she know you want to fuck Ransom?" Paul grinned.

"I don't want to fuck him! I want more —" I stopped and sighed, hanging my head. "Fuck."

"Don't worry. Your secret is safe with me, Sal. But if you think you're going to be able to resist Ransom in your house, you're wrong. You'll fuck up. So, again, I say: don't hurt him. He deserves someone who's going to love him out in the open."

"Am I that obvious? Even the bodyguard said something to me."

"Which one?"

"Um, Buster."

"Buster was an interrogator. He knows how to tell if someone is lying just by looking at them. He reads people."

"How do you know all this?"

"I've had a lot of time in here to read and think." Paul cocked a brow. "If you can't be out with him, let him be."

"Pfft. What makes you think Ransom even wants me?"

The door opened and Ransom sauntered in. He glanced from me, to Paul, and then smiled.

"I talked with your doctor and they're getting the ball rolling. I can come back on New Year's if you want? We can toast with grape juice."

"I think you should go out on the town, Ransom. How often are you in L.A. for New Year's?" Paul motioned to me. "I'm sure Sal knows all the good places to go."

"Oh, um, I wouldn't want to impose —" Ransom began.

"No worries, I'm sure Scarlett would love to hang with you," I assured him.

"Besides, I'll see you soon enough, right? You really don't need to babysit me, Ransom." Paul wrapped an arm around Ransom's shoulders and I shot him a look as he eyed me with mirth. "How often do you get to hang out with a big Hollywood movie star?"

"Okay, well, if you're really okay with it, Sal."

"Oh, I'm sure he is." Paul winked at me.

Fuck.

Chapter 3

By the time we got back to my house, I was sweating buckets. Between the bodyguard and Paul, I was seriously failing at keeping my crush on Ransom Fox a secret. Ransom jumped out of the car as I cut the engine. He waited for me by the front door, I unlocked it, and we entered. Scarlett was on the couch, feet curled beneath her, reading a script. I leaned over and kissed the top of her head.

"Hey, you." She glanced up at me. "Where have you been?"

"Taking Ransom on a tour of city."

"I made food. It's on the stove." Scarlett pushed my hip. "Go, I need to read."

"Yes, ma'am!" I headed to the kitchen and Ransom followed.

"I thought she was at the studio," Ransom said.

"She does her lines and they edit it onto the movie. When they film movies, they usually film scenes out of order."

"They do?" Ransom sat down at the kitchen island.

"Yup." I fixed Ransom a plate and then got one for myself. "This last movie I did, we filmed the end first."

"Your dad was in the movies, wasn't he?"

"Yes, he was. Both he and my mother were in films back in the day. My dad was a rising star in Italy before he and Mom moved to the U.S. They auditioned for a movie out here and were both hired. It skyrocketed from there. My dad changed his last name —"

"Wait, what? What was it?"

I leaned over the island and lowered my voice. "Falcon, but my dad thought Falco sounded cooler."

"I like Falcon."

"I do, too, but I left it Falco for my father."

"So, Salvatore Falcon." Ransom mulled it over. "I like it."

"I like Ransom Fox. Is that your real name?"

"Ransom is. I changed my last name."

"Oh, did you? Do tell."

"It's O'Donovan. A lot of information came out about Gareth and me so it's common knowledge now. We kept the fact that we were brothers secret for a long time to throw off our father. Things are good now, though."

"Why do I feel like there's a huge story there?"

"Because there is."

I studied Ransom's face. "I'll tell you a secret if you tell me something."

"Like what?"

"The first time I got in front of a camera for a sex scene, I almost cried."

"What? Why?"

"I was naked and so was she, save for the little stickies on her boobs and the mesh thongs we both wore. I was so nervous I practically threw up and we had to do the scene fifteen times before I actually pulled my shit together."

"I can't see you being nervous. You look like you have all your shit together when you're kissing your leading ladies."

"Well *now* I do." I laughed. "So, tell me something."

Ransom told me all about his childhood, his mother's death, and his father's spiral into drugs and how he and Gareth fought their way out. I was impressed. The guy was a fighter, which made me want him even more.

"But your dad's cool now?"

"Yes. He's clean. I mean, he still has some time to do on his sentence, but he's happy."

"He's happy in prison?" I cocked a brow.

"I know, sounds weird, huh? But he is. I went to see

him and he's healthy."

We finished eating and settled on the couch. I put Ransom's favorite movie in and we both reclined while watching it. I repeatedly snuck peeks at him. I couldn't believe he was in my house sitting right next to me. My phone chimed and I checked the caller ID. The director of my latest movie was calling. I answered.

"What's up, Steven?"

"We have a couple scenes we need you to come back in for. Can you be here in the morning?"

"It's New Year's Eve tomorrow. You do know that, right?"

"We're shooting in the morning, not at night. See you at six a.m."

The phone disconnected and I ran a hand through my hair with an irritated sigh.

"What's up?" Ransom asked.

"I have to go to the studio tomorrow. You want to come with?"

"Seriously? Hell, yes!"

"Then we better get some sleep."

Ransom leapt off the couch. "Night!"

I laughed.

I stood against the wall as the director barked out orders. Ransom was in awe, it seemed, at the lot we were shooting on. It looked like downtown Manhattan, complete with restaurants. One of my costars was getting ready for our scene. They applied blood to his shirt and a makeup artist worked movie magic to put a dark bruise around his eye.

"Okay, Sal! You know what you need to do!" my director shouted. "Be back in a sec." I winked at Ransom.

I took my marker and waited for the director to call 'action.' As soon as he did, I was in a full-out sprint. My costar was inches in front of me and I grabbed the tail of his shirt.

"Cut!"

I stopped and placed my hands on my knees, breathing slowly. I was dizzy and that was odd. A warm handed landed on my shoulder and I looked up to see Ransom, looking worried.

"You okay?" he asked.

"Yes."

"Take two!"

I groaned and tried to smile at Ransom. "You may regret coming now."

"Nah, I'll just go sit in your chair and look actorish."

"Is that a word?"

"Sure." Ransom winked and walked back to my director's chair.

We ended up doing the scene four times before the director was happy. I took Ransom back to the house so we could change for tonight's party. I was giddy about taking him out with me, even though I couldn't call him my date. God, I wanted him to be, though.

I walked out of the bathroom to find Scarlett on my bed, flipping through invitations with furrowed brows.

"What's up?" I asked, dropping my towel and rummaging through my underwear drawer.

Scarlett peered over her shoulder. "Wear the black briefs."

"Why?"

"Because if you and Ransom get naughty, he'll like them." Scarlett rolled over and eyed my ass. It's not like she'd never seen me naked, but she didn't normally stare. "What's that?"

"What?" I looked over my shoulder.

"Looks like a rash."

"I don't know. I wore the clothes from the set. Maybe they washed it in the wrong detergent?"

"How many times have you told them you can't have clothes washed in scented detergent?" Scarlett scowled.

"Did you look through the invitations?" I motioned to them on the bed.

"I did. I think I want to attend the party at the Viper Room."

I pulled on my briefs and looked at all the invitations. One of them caught my eye and I grinned.

"Do you mind if I take Ransom to Jasper Jamison's party?"

"The heavy metal guy? Ooh, he'd love that!" Scarlett bounced on the bed in glee.

"Why don't you come with us?" I asked.

"Sweetie, you're not going to get anywhere with Ransom Fox if I'm there. Let's be serious. I don't mind going by myself. I can always take a girlfriend."

"Scarlett, stop thinking something is going to happen. I'm telling you, Ransom Fox isn't gay."

"Okay, if you say so." Scarlett walked over to my closet and began shuffling through all my clothes. "Here, wear these jeans and this T-shirt."

"Not a suit?" I asked, confused.

"No suits! This is a hard-core rocker party, Sal."

"Okay, jeans and a T-shirt. Are you sure you're okay going by yourself? I don't want to leave you out."

"I'm choosing to go out by myself. Have fun, will

ya?" Scarlett blew me a kiss as she left my room. I stared in the mirror and hoped like hell I could make it through the night without kissing Ransom Fox.

Chapter 4

Sal went all out for me, getting a limo to drive us out to wherever he was taking me. He was being secretive as fuck. We pulled up to a huge house surrounded by palm trees. The front of the house was all glass and I stared up at it in awe. The limo driver opened the door and Sal stepped out first, extending a hand to me. We walked to the front door together and Sal knocked. The door opened seconds later and my mouth dropped open.

"Well, hell, Sal! You brought me a fellow rocker?"

"Jasper Jamison?" I practically whispered.

"And he fucking knows me! Awesome!"

Jasper grabbed my hand and yanked me into the house. I glanced over my shoulder to find Sal grinning as he walked behind us. Jasper led me into a large, open-air room. His awards lined one wall and there was a piano, drum kit, and keyboard against the far wall. The house was packed and Jasper led me around and introduced me to all his friends. I felt like a kid in a musical store. All my favorite guys were there and they were really nice. I looked for Sal and saw him standing against the bar, he winked and raised a glass to me.

"Ransom, you ever do karaoke?" Jasper asked me.

"Now and then. Why?"

"Every year, we get the guests to fill out a piece of paper with their favorite band and song, then we pass a hat around and whoever picks that song has to sing it."

"That could be interesting." I chuckled.

"So, you in?" Jasper nudged me.

I laughed and shook my head, looking at him. In that moment, I swore he reminded me of someone I knew. We headed to the bar and I leaned against it, glancing over at Sal.

"Thanks for bringing me here. I know you probably had a lot of parties to choose from."

"I knew you'd like this one."

"Don't let him fool you, Ransom. Sal comes to every party I have. He's a heavy metal junkie." Jasper wrapped an arm around Sal.

"Is that right?" I cocked a brow.

"So," Sal coughed. "You doing the hat again?"

"Yes, and here it comes. Hope you've had enough alcohol." Jasper chuckled.

The hat stopped in front of me and I reached in, moving a few pieces around before pulling a slip out. I unfolded it and read the band and song.

"Shit." I laughed.

"What did you get?" Sal leaned over. "Whitesnake, *Still of the Night.*"

"Good thing I know that one, eh?" I elbowed Sal playfully.

"Dude, that is the perfect song for you! You've got that rough voice. Fucking love it!" Jasper cackled.

We sat at the bar as one by one, the guests got up and sang whatever song they'd gotten stuck with. Jasper's guitarist, Liam, was singing George Michael's *Different Corner* and doing one hell of a job.

"This song always gave me goose bumps," Sal said in my ear.

"He's got fabulous range," I observed.

"Who? George Michael or Liam?" Sal snickered.

"Both."

The song ended and we all clapped and whistled. Jasper bounced up and took the microphone. "Come on, Ransom!"

"Already?" I laughed.

"Yep! Knock us out."

I stood by the floor-to-ceiling windows and held the

microphone to my lips. Jasper was cracking up next to me and Sal was right in front with all the other guests. I waited for my cue and went all out. Jasper was singing my back up and I stomped back and forth belting out the lyrics. Everyone was bouncing up and down, clapping and whistling. I stopped right in front of everyone and stared straight at Sal. The lyrics were so damn fitting for my situation. I wanted Sal Falco naked in my arms. I dropped to my knees as the song slowed down and leaned back, my head almost hitting the floor as I sang.

The crowd went crazy as I jumped back to my feet and Jasper and I rocked back and forth. I screamed into the microphone and the whole place was rocking. There wasn't any more room to stand on the floor and people were climbing on top of the bar. It was fucking crazy! People joined us and then Sal was right next to me, singing into the microphone. Jasper was clapping as the song came to an end and I handed him the mic.

"I have to say, in all my years, no one has done a better job than Ransom Fox! Give it up for Ransom!"

The partygoers went wild with applause and I bowed. "Thank you all so much!"

"I need a drink," Sal said.

"Me too."

We ended up on one of the biggest couches I've ever seen. It wrapped around the entire room. Jasper was sitting next to us, sipping his beer, and Sal was on the other side of me with water. I'd switched back to water about an hour ago. I didn't like getting drunk and I especially didn't want to get drunk around Sal on New Year's Eve, for fucks sake.

"It's almost midnight, my friends." Jasper took another swig of beer. "It's good to finally meet you, Ransom."

"I love your music. It's what made me and my brother want to play heavy metal."

"How is the youngest? Having kids yet?" Jasper winked.

"He and his husband are considering it, but I think it's going to be a bit longer. Gareth doesn't want kids until he can devote time to raising them."

"Yeah, well, I didn't plan on having any for that same reason, but over the years the drugs and alcohol clouded that."

"So, you have kids?" I asked in astonishment.

"I've got one for sure who I know of. His mother wouldn't let me see him, though, when he was growing up. I don't blame her. She said if I couldn't be there full-time, I couldn't be there at all. I was fucked up, though, drinking, smoking, doing heroin. I finally kicked the drugs and then I lost track of her. I have no idea where my kid is."

"So you have a son." I nodded.

"Yep. Kid looked just like me as a child. Wonder

what he looks like now?"

"Ever tried to find her?"

"I did." Jasper nodded. "Hired a private investigator and everything, but she must have changed her name."

Someone started counting down over by the bar and Jasper sprung from the couch.

"It's about that time!"

Sal and I both stood, counting down as well, and all the guests gathered around the middle of the room. I was having a great time, and when we got to 'one,' the woman next to me grabbed my face and kissed me. I turned from her and found Sal looking at me.

"Happy New Year, Sal!" I hugged him.

His arms circled me and I thought my whole body was going to liquify at his touch. He was warm and smelled so damned good — like cedar or something along those lines. I don't know what cologne he was wearing, but I was going to run out and buy some. People wanting to hug us pulled us apart, and as I got farther away from him, my body ached to be back in his embrace. Our eyes met across the room and a shiver ran down my spine at the look in his. Was I imagining it? Maybe.

We were back in the limo by three in the morning and I was exhausted. Sal handed me a bottle of water and I chugged it down. I could barely keep my eyes open as we drove through the city.

"Did you have fun?" Sal asked.

"I really did. Thank you so much for taking me."

"Jasper really liked you."

"He told me to come by any time. He's really cool."

The limo pulled into Sal's driveway and stopped. Sal got out first and extended his hand to me. I took it and stumbled on my way out, landing right in his arms. I peered up and cleared my throat.

"Sorry."

"No problem. You okay? A little tipsy, maybe?"

I was about to say no, but then realized I could use this to my advantage. I chuckled softly and ran a hand through my hair. "I might be a little. I don't drink very often."

"Well, let me help you inside then."

I mentally fist-pumped the air as Sal's arm wove around my middle, holding me firmly to his side. We entered the house and he navigated the long hall to the room I was staying in. I hit the bed face first once we got in and Sal chortled, removing my shoes.

"So tired," I mumbled into the comforter.

"I know, but you really have to get up so I can tuck you in."

"Can't move." I tilted my head to the side to see Sal walking toward the closet. Damn, he had a fine ass. He grabbed what looked like a down comforter and turned back to me. I closed my eyes as he unfolded it across my body. The bed dipped a bit and I cracked open one lid to see Sal sitting on the edge, smiling at me.

"What?" I asked softly.

"Need anything?"

I wanted to tell him I needed him, naked on top of me, but I wasn't going to. I wondered how fast he'd kick me out if he knew I wanted to pounce on him.

"Nah," I finally answered. "Just sleep."

I closed my eyes and buried my face in the pillow. I heard the light switching off and Sal moving around the room.

"Good night, Ransom. Happy New Year," he said quietly.

The door closed behind him and I sighed. My New Year's resolution was going to be getting over my crush on the man.

Chapter 5

SAL

I woke up to see Scarlett on the side of the bed smiling wide. She handed me a cup of coffee and sat cross-legged in front of me. I know what she wanted to hear, that I'd made a move on Ransom. I wish I had, but I didn't have the brass balls to do it. I exhaled and closed my eyes, shaking my head.

"Oh, Sal." Scarlett shook her head.

"I know, okay. Don't make it worse. We had fun and he hugged me at midnight."

"Well, he's down at the beach this morning."

"How do you know?"

"Left a note on the counter. He was going to see Paul and then go."

"Shit!" I jumped out of bed and ran for the bathroom.

"What is it?"

"I should be with him! I can show him all the stuff!"

"I think he thought you'd like to sleep in."

I ran back out of the bathroom, threw some old cargo shorts on, and rifled through my T-shirts. I grabbed my phone as I attempted to put both on while hopping around trying to secure a flip-flop. I dialed Ransom and he answered on the second ring.

"Hello?"

"Hey! Um, Scarlett just told me you've gone down to the beach?"

"I'm still at the hospital, I was getting ready to go —"

"Why don't I meet you at the Santa Monica Pier? I can take you to the aquarium?"

"You don't have to, Sal."

"I know. It'll be fun, right? I need to get out." Scarlett snorted and I threw my other flip-flop at her.

"Sure, okay. Um, where do we meet?"

"I'll meet you right in front of the aquarium, say in about an hour?"

"Okay, sure!"

"See you then!" I hung up and collapsed on the bed. My flip-flop hit me in the head and I glanced up to see Scarlett smiling. "Oh, stop."

"Have fun!" Scarlett wiggled her fingers at me and left the room.

I drove to Santa Monica, barely able to keep my shit together. I wanted to spend as much time with Ransom as possible. Did that make me pathetic? Probably, but I didn't care. Scarlett was always quick to point out that I could have any woman or man I wanted, but I only wanted one. I was hooked from the second I set eyes on Ransom Fox. I finally found parking and secured my baseball hat and sunglasses. I wandered around the pier until I saw Ransom leaning against the wooden railing, staring out over the ocean. He was wearing cargo shorts as well, but he had on sneakers and a long-sleeved T-shirt. I just stood there for a minute, staring at him. I couldn't help it. It was chilly out, maybe in the upper sixties, and I shivered a bit as I walked toward him.

"Hey."

Ransom turned and smiled. "Hey. Nice disguise."

"I know, I'm so stealthy." I chuckled. I extended a hand toward the aquarium and he began to walk ahead of me.

"You really don't need to babysit me, Sal. I'm sure you have a lot to do."

"I really don't. I'm between projects right now, so I have free time. I never get to do any of this stuff anymore."

We entered the aquarium and I glanced around with a grin. It'd been years since I'd come. I'd gotten so busy with my career, I hadn't taken much time off lately. I paid the admission fee for both of us and Ransom arched his brows at me.

"I plan on paying today, so don't bother arguing."

"Fine by me." Ransom grinned.

Christ, he was so damned gorgeous. I cleared my throat and walked ahead of him. We stopped at the touch tanks and Ransom peered in, staring at all the colorful fish.

"I can touch these?" he asked.

"Yep."

"I'm having a flashback to a movie I just saw." Ransom chuckled.

"Which one?"

"Cartoon. I'm thinking all these guys are cringing and screaming."

"Come on," I laughed. "Let's see the rest of the stuff."

We sat in on story time and I could tell Ransom was very interested. The aquarium was small, nothing like other ones I'd been to, but it was worth it as far as I was concerned. Once we were done, I walked with Ransom down the pier.

"Is that a roller coaster?" Ransom pointed ahead.

"Yep, and there's a Ferris wheel and an old-fashioned carousel."

"Can we, I mean, do you think we can go on the rides?"

I glanced over at Ransom to see him blushing slightly. It was endearing, and I wanted to hug him.

"Hell, yes," I answered. He looked over at me with a small smile.

"You must think I'm a kid, huh?"

"Why would I think that?"

"Because I'm thirty and I want to ride the coaster."

"I'm going to ride all the rides," I said seriously.

"Are you fucking with me?"

"Nope! Hurry up!" I laughed, running down the pier.

We jumped on the bumper cars first — well, not cars, but they bumped into each other. I slammed into the back of Ransom's and he whipped around, coming at me full throttle. His laughter was music to my ears as we continued to plow into one another.

We went from ride to ride and I laughed as Ransom let out a childlike scream on the roller coaster. I put my hands in the air and just enjoyed the cool wind against my face. Ransom's hand gripped my shirt and I opened my eyes, looking at him. His eyes were closed and he was burrowed into my side.

"You can't enjoy it if you're not seeing it!" I shouted.

"I'm good!" he shouted back.

I chortled and put an arm around him, pulling him in close. Who would have thought Ransom Fox was afraid of coasters?

"Why did you want to come on the coaster if you're afraid of them?"

"I'm trying to get over my fear!"

"Well, hiding isn't going to do it!" I gently eased Ransom out of my side and turned his face forward as we crested another hill. "Keep your eyes open and look at the beauty surrounding you!"

The car went over the hump and then we were falling. Ransom was screaming again and I don't think I've laughed that hard in years. Once the ride came to a stop, Ransom teetered off and found the railing, inhaling deeply. He glanced up and grinned.

"Let's do it again!"

I laughed.

We rode the coaster over and over until Ransom was screaming in delight and not fear. I took him on all of the rides, including the Ferris wheel and the carousel. The day had somehow gotten away from us and we were back on the Ferris wheel for the thousandth time that day as the sun was setting. The sky was rose-orange and Ransom's cheeks were pink from the cold. He was giddy, couldn't sit still in the seat, and pointing to everything around us. I couldn't remember a day when I'd been so happy. Ransom turned to me just then and grinned.

"I'm hungry. You want to get something to eat when

we get down?"

"Sounds good."

Ransom took my hand and my whole body exploded at his proximity. His mere touch filled me with desire.

"Thank you for doing this for me. I've been so stressed out lately, I forgot how to have fun. Between Paul, Gareth, and the new album, I haven't been taking very good care of myself."

"Well, I'm glad to be of service."

Ransom shot me a thousand-watt smile and I wanted to pounce on him. The ride made a full circle around and we got off. I held on to the metal guardrail and took a deep breath.

"Sal? You okay?"

"Yeah, just a little motion sickness maybe. Let's find that food!"

We ended up at a seafood place on the piers and I ordered shrimp. I think Ransom ordered the whole menu. I had no idea where he put all the food he consumed. Ransom ordered and caught me staring at him.

"What?"

"I have no idea how you pack that much food in. I have to work out five times a week to look like you." I shook my head with a smile. "Must have an awesome metabolism."

"I guess so. I never really worried about my weight

and just ate what I wanted. Jinx hates me for that."

"Jinx Jett? Your drummer?"

"Yep. Jinx used to be a little overweight back in the day. He had a serious obsession with blueberry muffins."

"I'm all about the cannoli. My mom makes them from scratch."

"Is that a dessert?" Ransom asked.

My eyes widened. "You've never had one?"

"Well, I've had Italian food before. Not sure if I've had a cannoli."

"Yeah, it's a dessert. The best one."

Our food arrived and I dove in. I loved shrimp no matter how it was cooked and could eat it all day every day. I realized it had gotten quiet and glanced up to find Ransom smiling at me.

"What?" I asked around a mouthful of shrimp.

"You really don't need to play babysitter, Sal. I'm a big boy and can navigate around L.A. and its surrounding areas."

"Like I said, I've got free time right now, and I don't want to spend it sitting at home."

"Okay, fine." Ransom folded his hands on the table. "Can we see the Hollywood sign?"

"Yep. I'll take you on a drive to get closer."

"No, I mean I want to touch it." Ransom grinned.

"Um, yeah, that's a no. I can take you on a hike and

you can get close, but no touching. They consider that trespassing."

"Aw, come on!" Ransom chuckled. "Big movie star like you? I bet they'd let you touch it."

I leaned forward and lowered my voice. "I almost got arrested for touching it."

"What? When?" Ransom's eyes bulged.

"After my first huge movie break and I was on every damn cover of every magazine you could think of. I went up there and was going to have Scarlett take a picture of me touching the sign. Yep, we got back down to a waiting squad car and we both got a good talking to."

I searched Ransom's face just then. He seemed, I don't know... sad? "Hey, what's wrong?" Ransom gave me a barely-there smile and I took one of his hands. "Talk to me. What did I say?"

"It's nothing, I promise," he assured me, removing his hand from mine.

"I really am sorry you can't touch it, but maybe we can take a picture that makes it look like you are?"

"Okay, sure." Ransom shot me a grin.

"Well, it looked more like a grimace, but maybe I was seeing way too much into it. We finished dinner and walked back out to the parking lot. Ransom walked toward his car and I headed to mine.

"So, I'll see you back at my place?"

Ransom looked back me and nodded. "Sure."

I stood in the parking lot and watched him leave. What the hell had happened during dinner that made his whole attitude change? I mean I *could* get him up to the sign to touch it. Hell — if it put that smile back on his face, I'd go to jail for Ransom Fox.

Fuck.

I was so screwed.

Chapter 6

The alarm on my phone woke me up. I was going to see Paul again today and hopefully get his papers in order. Everything moved at a snail's pace over at the hospital and they informed me the day before that they'd lost his transfer paperwork. I got up and showered, getting dressed quietly. I was going to get food on my way over to see Paul and I really didn't want to run into Sal or his gorgeous girlfriend.

I went straight to my room after I got back to Sal's last night, complaining of a headache. I felt like shit because he'd looked like I'd kicked his puppy or something. Truth was I didn't want to hear about Scarlett and him. I hated any reminder that Sal was straight. I wanted him for me. Fuck. Why did I have to want him so much? He was absolutely perfect in every way — well, to me he was.

I grabbed my wallet and threw a hat on as I left the bedroom. I tiptoed through the living room and heard a cough from the kitchen. Sal's house was open — meaning the kitchen was in full view of the living room. I looked over to see Scarlett at the kitchen island. Her hair was up loosely in a bun and she didn't have a bit of makeup on. Sad thing was that she still looked gorgeous.

"Oh, uh, hey." I waved. "I didn't want to wake anyone."

"Sneaking out?" She arched her brows.

"Oh! No, I mean, not really. I'm going to visit my friend Paul. Could you let Sal know I'll be back this afternoon for our hike?"

"Sure thing, sweetie." She smiled.

I hurried out to the driveway and jumped into my tiny rental car. I drove to the highway and cursed at the bumper-to-bumper traffic. By the time I got to the hospital, it was already nine in the morning. I pulled up and parked, got out and stopped in my tracks as I noticed Buster standing outside on the phone. Was the man everywhere?

"Buster." I nodded as I walked by him.

"Call you back." Buster stuck his phone in his back pocket and eyed me from head to toe. "You look a little sunburned. Too much fun at the piers?"

"What the hell? You were there?"

"Of course I was. You looked like you were having fun."

"Ugh!" I threw my hands up and walked round him.

"Make sure you have good shoes for that hike today."

I turned around and stared at him. "What?"

"Oh, and you can touch the sign. I made it happen." Buster grinned.

"I hate you," I grumbled as I opened the door to the hospital.

"No, you don't!" Buster called after me.

I headed to Paul's room, signing a few autographs along the way. Everyone at the hospital had been sworn to secrecy about Paul being there, so signing a few pieces of paper now and then wouldn't kill me. I was surprised it hadn't gotten out what Paul had done, although I guess I shouldn't have been with Mac Collins and his security team on our side. I knocked on Paul's door and heard the 'come in' from the other side. I pushed the door open and stopped in my tracks. Paul was dressed from the waist down, his muscular chest gleaming with sweat.

"Oh, should I come back?" I asked.

Paul's blue eyes zeroed in on me and I felt caught ogling him. He grinned and wiped his temple with his forearm. I couldn't believe how ripped he was. I mean, he wrestled in high school and he was pretty well built then, but now? This was a whole new ball of wax I hadn't been prepared for.

"Nah, come on in. I'm just finishing up." Paul stepped into the bathroom and splashed some water on his face.

"You work out a lot?" I asked stupidly.

"Well, I'm kind of stuck here, you know? Not much to do around here but eat, sleep and shit."

I sat down with a sigh and peered up at him from under my lashes. "I'm sorry."

"Hey." Paul crossed the room to me and squatted in front of me. "Don't *ever* apologize, got it? I needed to be in here."

"I just feel — I mean, can you even leave here?"

"What do you mean? Like a trip to Disneyland?" Paul smirked.

"No, I mean just out, for lunch or something?"

"I could ask my doctor. I'm sure he'd let me. Why? You feel like going out?"

"I'd just feel better if we got out of here for a couple of hours."

"Well, let me shower and then I'll find him, okay?" Paul stood and all I could see was his happy trail. I swallowed hard and glanced up at him. He was smiling at me.

"What?" I asked.

"Nothing. See you in a few?"

"Um, sure. I can meet you in the lobby."

I wandered around the hospital grounds for a bit, just waiting for Paul. I walked out into the courtyard and looked around at all the foliage along with the multiple ponds and waterfalls. It *was* peaceful here. Other patients were wandering around, sitting in the grass, playing croquet, or reading under one of the many large trees. I crossed the grass to one of the ponds and sat on a rock near it. Large colorful fish swam around, all rushing to where I was sitting. Probably looking for food.

"That's my favorite one."

I stood up quickly and whirled around. Paul was standing behind me. He was in jeans with sneakers and a T-shirt.

"Shit. I was supposed to meet you in the lobby."

"It's cool. I figured if you weren't there, you'd be out here." Paul raised his face to the sun. "It's nice out here, huh?"

"Do you spend a lot of time out here?"

"Yeah. Pretty much every morning after my run I come sit out here. The fish and I are good friends." Paul winked. "I got the green light from the doctor. He just needs you to sign me out."

"Okay. Where did you want to go?"

"As long as there's food, I don't care." Paul snickered. "I've gotten tired of vanilla pudding and lime Jell-O." He noticed my face and took my hand. "Shit, it seems like I'm saying all the wrong things."

"No, I'm okay." I inhaled slowly, letting it out just as

slow. "Okay, let's get out of here."

I signed Paul out and we walked into the parking lot. I looked for Buster but didn't see him. Paul slid into the passenger seat and folded his hands in his lap. I shut the door and he flinched. I took his hands and searched his face.

"What is it?"

"I'm just nervous. I'm afraid to be out."

"Hey, from what I hear you're doing very well, Paul. They've changed your meds and your doc says you're progressing by leaps and bounds."

"Thanks." Paul looked around warily. "Can we go?"

"Sure. I'll find someplace nearby."

"Maybe we can go to the beach?"

"Sure."

I drove out to Hermosa and we walked along the shoreline, eating breakfast burritos. Paul didn't want to be around a lot of people, and according to my GPS and a few search apps, Hermosa wasn't as busy as Santa Monica this time of year. As we walked along the beach, I could tell the app was right. Maybe a handful of people were out this morning, probably because it was in the sixties. We took the trail to the pier and walked to the end of it. A few people were fishing, and other than the occasional screeching seagull, it was quiet. Paul and I sat down on the wooden pier planks and watched the waves roll up onto shore.

"I'm sorry, Ransom." Paul said quietly.

"For what?" I looked over at him.

"What I did, what I said, everything I've done. I know I've said it before, but I don't feel right about all of it. I know I'm sick, but I don't feel like I deserve your kindness — or Gareth's. I *was* in love with you back then, sometimes I feel like I still am, but I would have never hurt Gareth."

"I wanted to thank you, Paul," I said softly.

"What the hell for?" He turned to me with incredulous eyes.

"You saved me and Gareth that night. You told them to take us first while you sat behind the wheel with your hand crushed. I know it's our fault you sustained such a bad injury. If you'd been able to get blood flow to your fingers, it wouldn't have been so bad."

Paul turned to me and cupped my face in his hands. "I would do it all over again, Ransom. Don't you ever think I wouldn't. I didn't realize it had gotten this bad with me until I started to think things that I never would have. I should have gotten help a lot sooner."

"I should have seen it, but I was so wrapped up in my own life I didn't stop to see if you were okay."

"Don't ever feel bad, okay? I'm getting the help I need now and you guys are doing so damned good! I'm so fucking proud of you, Ransom." Paul released my face and leaned back against the railing. "Let's change the subject.

How's your stay with Sal?"

"I don't know if we should talk about that," I admitted.

"Hey, I care about you, Ransom. I just want you to be happy, and if Sal makes you happy, then I want to hear about it."

I eyed him sideways. "Can I be honest right now?"

"Sure."

"Damn, you filled out nice."

Paul threw his head back and let out a hearty laugh. I busted out too, doubling over in a fit of laughter.

"I thought you were staring at me a little too close," Paul choked out.

"Well, hell! I walk in and you look like that?"

We laughed until we cried. Paul wiped at his eyes and threw an arm around my shoulders. "We are fucking bent."

"I do love you, Paul."

"I know, as a brother. As it should be." He got serious and searched my eyes. "You have a thing for Sal."

"What? No I don't."

"Ransom." Paul arched his brows.

"Is it that obvious?"

"Nah, I just know you. He'd be lucky to have you, Ransom."

"Oh sure, if he was gay. I'm stuck in that house with

him and his girlfriend and I want to hate her but she's so damned nice!"

"I think things will work out for you, Ransom. You're going to get your happy ending."

"I think you will too, Paul. You're going to find that one guy who makes you whole."

"Yeah? I hope so."

I texted Sal and waited for him on the trail up to the Hollywood sign. The sky was clear blue and there was a slight breeze. I felt better about Paul now. In the beginning, I wanted him rotting in prison for what he tried to do to Gareth, for the harm he did cause psychologically. But now? I just wanted him to get better and have a life. I knew he'd be back in the band in some way when he was ready to come back.

Family protects family.

Footsteps sounded from behind me and I turned to find Sal walking up the trail to me. He looked fabulous in sweats, a tight shirt, and sneakers. A small pack rested on his back. His hair was product free and waving gently in the breeze.

"Hey," he said as he reached me. "How was your morning?"

"I spent it with Paul in Hermosa."

"How is he doing?"

"Ready to get home. I don't blame him. We'll be able to see him a lot more once he's moved back to Arizona."

"Good. You ready for this?"

"Yep. Lead the way."

We hiked up the trail and my thighs and ass were burning. I'd hiked quite a few places in Arizona, so this was a lot easier on me. Sal stopped and removed a bottle of water from the small pack on his back. He sipped it and handed it to me. We were halfway to the top and I needed to conserve my energy.

"This must be easy on you, huh?" Sal said, resuming our hike.

"Well, considering that Flagstaff is seven-thousand feet elevation? Yeah, this is child's play."

We finally reached the top and I stood in awe at the view in front of me. We could see right over the top of the sign and it was gorgeous.

"Wow!"

"California's not so bad when you see it from up here."

"Do you really like it here?"

"I've lived here for a long time and there have been

times when I wanted to move."

"Yeah? Where to? New York?"

"Arizona, actually," Sal answered.

"You're kidding, right?" I stared at him.

"Nope. It's a close enough commute by airplane if I really wanted to do it. Sebastian's been talking about moving one of his studios out there. It's cheaper by far."

"That would be cool," I said seriously.

"Well —" Sal took a look around. "If you want to touch the sign, now would be the time."

"I'm not going to do it, but I will take a selfie."

"What? Why not?"

"I think I'll show respect for it and not lay my grubby hands on it."

"There may be hope for you yet, Ransom Fox." Sal chuckled.

"You defiled it." I narrowed my eyes at him.

"I didn't hump it! I stuck a finger on it."

"Who knows where that finger had been?"

"Asshole." Sal chortled. "Get in front of it and I'll take a picture."

"Come with me, we'll take one together."

Sal stood next to me and I held my phone up as he put his arm around my shoulders. I couldn't believe I was standing in front of the Hollywood sign with one of the biggest movies stars on the planet. I snapped the picture and put my phone back in my pocket.

"I can't thank you enough for this, Sal."

"You're very welcome. What do you want to do tonight? Want to go to an exclusive club that no one can get into?"

"How about we watch a movie and hang out?"

"Are you sure you don't want me to take you somewhere you've never been? I can get us in to any restaurant."

I turned to look at him and smiled. "I think you'll figure out pretty quickly I'm a homebody. I like hanging out with my friends just fucking around on the guitar or watching a football game. I'm pretty low maintenance. Shit, we could eat at Micky-Dees and I'd be good."

"Low-key, got it." Sal nodded.

"Ready to head back?"

"Yep."

By the time we got back to Sal's, the sun had set. I went to take a shower, as did Sal. I hopped out and wiped the mirror, checking myself out. I fingered my hair and walked out into the room to get some clothes. I heard voices in the other room and tilted my head, trying to listen. Sal and Scarlett were talking about something and she did not sound happy. I threw on my sweats and a shirt and walked out to the living room. Scarlett stopped mid-sentence and smiled at me.

"Hey, Ransom. I was just telling Sal I was heading out to a friend's house tonight. You guys have fun!"

"You don't have to leave because of me," I said quickly. "If you and Sal just want to hang I can keep myself busy."

"Don't you worry about it." She winked at me.

Sal turned to me as Scarlett left and I walked over to the couch, settling in. "I'm sorry if I'm taking up your time. You really should spend some time with your girlfriend."

"Scarlett and I have been together for a long time. Trust me, she doesn't hold any ill will toward you, and she likes to do things on her own."

"Okay. I just don't want to cause any problems between the two of you."

"Believe me, you're not. So? What are we watching?"

"Um, how about *Devil in the Sky*?"

"Another one of mine? Don't you want to watch something else?"

"Nope. That's one of my favorites."

Sal chuckled and I'm pretty sure pre-cum dribbled out my dick. This man turned me on more than any man had in my past. I was excited/scared/turned on whenever I saw him. I needed to get over my feelings for the guy.

And fast.

Chapter 7

I woke up and immediately went for a run around the neighborhood. Hollywood Hills was exactly how I pictured it — ritzy. I ran out to the hiking trail and took it for miles, just trying to get out all my frustration. By the time I got back, Sal was standing in the kitchen sipping coffee and reading the morning paper.

"Hey, have a good run?" he asked.

"I did. How did you know?"

"Well, you're covered in sweat. Why don't you shower and then join me for breakfast?"

"Sure. Thanks for cooking again, by the way."

"Yep." Sal nodded, sticking his nose back in the paper.

I headed back to the guest room and jumped in the shower. I wanted to jack off, but felt like that wouldn't be right, jacking off in my crush's home. That made me chuckle and I finished washing up. I pulled on some sweats and a T-shirt and left my room.

I walked down the hall and stopped. Something felt off, like I was drunk or on a cruise ship in bad weather. Then the shaking began and I realized what it was. My skin broke out in a fine sheen of sweat as the shaking got harder.

"Ransom!" Sal shouted.

"In the hall! Oh my God, is it an earthquake?"

"Yes!" Sal turned the corner and grabbed my hand, hauling me into a doorframe.

"Oh my God, oh my God, oh my God…" I babbled.

"Ransom, look at me." Sal lifted my face to his. "It's okay, all right? It's not even a five."

Pictures fell off the walls and glass scattered everywhere. I hid in Sal's neck as the house seemed to rock back and forth. I was starting to feel sick from the rolling. I'd never experienced an earthquake. What if the house slid down the hill?

"Ransom, it's okay," Sal said soothingly.

"It's not stopping! Why isn't it stopping?" I shouted in a panic.

"It'll stop soon, I promise." Sal gently rubbed my back.

A loud groan came from the house as the shaking rocked us. A bookcase in the room fell over, spewing books across the floor, and a lamp fell over, shattering instantly. I vaguely heard something like a scream leave my lips and then Sal was holding my face in his hands.

"Ransom! Look at me!"

"Make it stop," I pleaded on almost a sob.

"Dammit!" Sal lunged forward and captured my lips.

Fingers threaded into my hair as Sal's tongue licked at my bottom lip. I opened up, wrapping my arms around his neck and kissing him back. I plastered my back to the doorframe as Sal Falco kissed me as though I were a woman in his arms instead of a man. The shaking finally stopped and the floor moved in a slow roll. Sal broke from the kiss and looked up at the ceiling. He looked back at me with a small smile.

"See? It stopped."

I had no idea what to say just then. My movie idol had just kissed me. The one man I had been in love with since I was twelve. I'd never looked at another man because the one I wanted was standing right in front of me. My mouth opened and then closed, then opened again.

"Ransom? I'm sorry I did that. I wanted you to calm down."

I was so far from calm it was ridiculous. I licked my lips and dove at Sal like my life depended on it. I slid a hand into his hair and palmed his cheek with the other as I kissed him. Sal didn't move for about two seconds and then he threw me down on the floor. I spread my legs, welcoming his weight and body heat.

"Fuck, I wanted this," Sal panted between kisses.

"Stop talking." I gripped his nape and pulled him back to my lips.

I arched my hips and groaned at Sal Falco's taste. My dick was practically screaming for freedom and then it bumped Sal's erection. I gasped and our lips parted. Sal's eyes held a look of absolute need and I'm sure it matched mine. I wanted him anywhere I could get him. The front door opened and Scarlett's voice floated across the house.

"Sal! Are you okay?"

"In the hall, Scarlett," Sal answered. He rose slowly and extended a hand to me. I took it and he pulled me up. Scarlett came around the corner and eyed us both.

"Well, now." She tapped her foot. "Did you get him into bed? If so —" she motioned around the house, " — that was some crazy sex."

What. The. Fuck? I glanced from Scarlett to Sal. Sal's face was beet red and Scarlett had a Cheshire cat smile. I felt like a homewrecker.

"Scarlett." Sal sighed audibly.

"Seriously, are you two okay?" she asked.

"I might have panicked just a little," I admitted sheepishly.

"No worries, cutie. My first earthquake scared the shit out of me. I cried and hid under my bed and it was only a three point one."

"What was this one?" Sal asked.

"Just shy of five. Packed a punch though, huh?" Scarlet sidled up next to me and took my face in her hands. "You've got some stubble burn there, hon. Sal, what did I say about shaving?"

"Scarlett." Sal warned.

"Did I just land in some other dimension? Your boyfriend kissed me and you're making jokes about it?" I gasped.

"He's still in shock, sweetie." Scarlett pushed my hair back from my temple and smiled. "I'm not really his girlfriend."

"Scarlett! Jesus!"

"Oh come on, Sal! Look at his lips and face! I'm not blind. You finally got a taste of Ransom Fox."

"Oh, fuck." Sal slid to the floor, holding his face.

"What is going on?" I practically shouted at them both. "I don't like being out of the loop and I hate when people make me feel stupid!"

"Sal?" Scarlett stared at him on the floor.

"I'll tell him." Sal sighed audibly.

"I'll start cleaning." Scarlett threw me a look and smiled. "Go easy on him, huh? He's had a crush on you for years."

"Oh for fucks sake!" Sal threw his hands up.

Scarlett chuckled and left us alone. I stared at Sal, trying to make sense of what was happening. I wasn't an idiot and an idea was forming in my head.

"The guys were right. She's your beard, isn't she?"

Sal stood and smoothed out his shirt. He motioned to me and then down the hall. I followed him and we went into the room I was occupying and he shut the door. I paced as I waited for him to speak.

"Scarlett is a really good friend. We met ten years ago at a movie audition and she knew right away I was gay. She's been keeping my secret all this time."

"Why did you kiss me?" I asked.

"I couldn't help myself. You're the only man I've ever wanted to cross that line for."

"Wait... what?"

"I've wanted you from the first time I ever saw your picture. The first time I saw you in concert I wanted to run up there and throw you down on the stage. The night we talked at Sebastian's, I wanted to borrow his room and do things to you that are illegal in some countries."

"You... want me?"

"For as long as I can remember, Ransom."

"This is surreal." I sat on the bed in a daze. Sal Falco wanted me?

"I'm sorry I kissed you. I just couldn't help it. I've wanted to do that for so long."

I started to chuckle and then it became full-out hysterical laughter. Sal Falco had wanted me for years? What were the fucking odds?

"Well, at least you're laughing and not punching me." Sal lightly laughed.

"Seriously? Did you not feel me reciprocating that kiss? Did I not grab you and lay one on you?" I stood and crossed the room to him.

"Meaning? I thought maybe I just got you at a bad time. You were freaked out —"

I grabbed Sal by the front of his shirt and hauled him into my arms. His face registered shock as I leaned in and locked eyes.

"I've wanted you since I was a kid, Sal. I've wanted you naked, under me, writhing in pleasure."

"Holy fuck," Sal whispered, his pupils taking over all color in his eyes.

"It will definitely be a religious experience." I nipped at his bottom lip.

"Is this real? Did I die in the quake and now my fantasy is coming true?"

"Really? I'm your fantasy?" I searched his eyes.

"I want you to be my everything, Ransom," Sal admitted softly.

I kissed him then because *fuck*, I couldn't believe those words had come out of his mouth. Sal wrapped his arms around me and gave in to me. I let my hand trail down his spine and onto his ass. I gripped it, pulling him closer to me. Sal gasped in my mouth and I grinned, pulling away slowly. I had no idea where all my bravado had come from. I was a man virgin just like Gareth had been. I'd only been with women, but I wanted Sal like no other. We broke from the kiss, both of us panting slightly.

"I haven't been with anyone for a while, Ransom." Sal regarded me nervously.

"Well, I haven't been with a man at all. Well, that's not true. I did kiss Paul a couple times in high school." I caressed Sal's cheek. "But I've always wanted you."

"This is so... can I thank the earthquake? Is that possible?"

"I think we should both thank it, but on that note, does that happen often?"

"It has been more recently. Another reason why I've been thinking of relocating before California drops into the ocean."

"And then Arizona is beachfront property." I waggled my eyebrows.

Sal grinned and then sobered. "We have a lot to talk about."

"Yes, we do. I never thought you were gay and it's obvious you want to keep it that way."

Sal sighed and paced the room. "I've been hiding

who I am my whole life! This industry *is* changing, but I've built my reputation as a ladies man, the leading man in all kinds of romantic movies. I'm so afraid of what will happen if I come out. I've been lying all this time."

"I'm not going to ask you to come out," I said quietly. Sal's head snapped to me and his eyes widened.

"You're not?"

"No. We don't even know where this is going. We have to get to know each other beyond Sal Falco and Ransom Fox. I mean, how much do we really know about each other? I know you like eggs and bacon."

"You know a lot more than most people do, Ransom. I thought for sure you'd see right through me. Paul did, and so did that Buster guy."

"They did?" I shook my head with a grin.

"Paul knew the second I walked into his room and Buster knew just by looking at me."

"Well that *is* his job." I smirked.

"It's his job to spot gay men?"

"I'm sure it's one of them," I snickered. I took his hand and pulled him to me. "Let's just take this one day at a time, okay? I'm going to be moving Paul within the next couple days, so let's spend that time getting to know each other better."

"That sounds like a plan." Sal nodded.

"But in the meantime." I arched a brow and pressed

my lips to his.

I almost sighed at how right it felt, as if I'd been waiting for this feeling and I finally found it. I teased his mouth open with my tongue and a low groan rumbled from my throat as Sal's arms wrapped around me, holding me close. We both took our time, slowly investigating each other — tongues sliding erotically against each other. I broke from the kiss first, panting a little. This man turned me on beyond belief. Our eyes met and my stomach did some weird flop thing as he grinned at me. There was a soft knock on the door and Sal crossed the room to open it. Scarlett stood there with a mile wide grin.

"Now that you two are done sucking face and all, can I get some help?"

I laughed.

Chapter 8

Ransom and I kept darting looks at each other as we cleaned the house up. The paintings incurred the most damage when they fell off the wall, and a few knick-knacks here and there were lost. All in all, it hadn't been too bad. Ransom handed over a large piece of glass from one of my frames and I chucked it into the trashcan I was lugging around. He brushed my hand and a tingle spread down my spine, pooling in my nuts. I couldn't keep my eyes off of him. He was just so… gorgeous.

I'd had plenty of fans say they loved me, but they only saw what was on the outside. I was attracted to intelligence and personality and Ransom had those in spades. He grinned at me just then, as if knowing what I was thinking. I wanted to take him somewhere special; somewhere I'd never taken anyone else. I wanted to share something with him no one else knew about, not even

Scarlett.

Once we got most of the house cleaned up, we reclined on the sofa with wine and I put an arm on the back of the couch behind Ransom. He leaned into me, his body heat shooting lust throughout my whole body. His scent was downright intoxicating. I wanted to bottle that shit.

"So, now what?" Scarlett eyed the two of us on the couch.

"Now we rebuild," I joked.

"Worst line in a movie ever." Ransom rolled his eyes.

"I think I know to which movie you are referring." Scarlett arched a brow. "And, please, as if that boat wouldn't have had any trouble navigating through all that debris."

"Let's not forget driving up a tsunami wave," I added.

"Okay, all kidding aside, what are you two going to do now?" she asked.

"We've agreed to get to know one another and take it slow," Ransom answered. "I'm not expecting Sal to come out for me. I know what he'd be giving up to do so."

"Trust me, Ransom. Sal and I have argued over this for years — the last two being the most brutal. There are so many gay actors out there now! No one is going to care."

"It's not just that I'm gay, Scarlett! I've always identified as straight to the media. What's going to happen when I suddenly hit the red carpet with Ransom on my arm? What are you going to say? They'll trash you for keeping my secret. You're just as guilty as I am."

"Don't worry about me, sweetie, I can hold my own. I'm not some feeble woman who will cry when the media chases me down. They're going to get a nice shot of my middle finger up their ass."

Ransom choked in laughter and Scarlett merely winked at him.

"I'm no newbie and I don't take shit from anyone."

"I can see why you two have gotten along all these years." Ransom beamed at me.

"She's been my rock when I was at my lowest," I agreed. "I'll always love her in a special way."

"Okay, now you're talking like I died or something." Scarlett stood and cracked her neck from side to side. "I'm going out for a drink. You two talk and get to know one another."

Scarlett kissed the top of my head and headed out. I turned on the couch and regarded Ransom. God, I'd always wanted him there. I realized the sun was starting to set. Where had the time gone?

"You want to grab some dinner? I want to take you somewhere."

"Sure."

I leaned over and kissed his lips gently. They were so

warm, so pliable, I found myself leaning in for more. Ransom allowed me in, his arms wrapping around my waist and pulling us closer. I couldn't think with him in my arms, his taste invading my mouth. I needed so much more from him. I broke from the kiss, barely keeping it together.

"We should go," I almost rasped.

"Okay."

We headed out to my favorite taco truck and I took Ransom down to a secluded stretch of beach. I owned the house right above it and I only came out here when I needed a break from everything. We sat in the cool sand and ate. It was quiet. A seagull screeched above us now and then, diving in to see if we'd give them any food.

"See the house behind us?"

Ransom glanced over his shoulder. "Yes."

"It's mine. I bought it when I first moved out here, before I became who I am now. No one knows about it, not even Scarlett. It's where I come when I want to get away from it all."

"And you're telling me about it," Ransom said slowly.

"I want you to think of it as yours too."

"Sal —"

"Don't, okay? I feel things for you I haven't felt for anyone, Ransom. It scares me."

"I know. I feel the same way," Ransom admitted. He stood and offered me his hand. "Come on. Show me the place."

I led Ransom into the house and he stopped in the living room. I heard a small gasp from Ransom and grinned. Every CD they'd ever made was sitting by my stereo and right above it was a picture of the band. Ransom turned around and arched a brow at me.

"You weren't lying."

"No. I wasn't." I closed the distance between us and took him into my arms. He melted into my embrace and opened up to me immediately. I loved how responsive he was to my kisses — my touch. A soft moan left his throat as I ran my hand down to his ass, cupping one cheek. I wanted him so badly I could fucking taste it. I moved us to the couch and followed Ransom down as he laid out on it. I didn't want to go too fast with him, but fuck I wanted to see what he was packing. I gripped his dick through the denim of his jeans and groaned at the size of his cock. I wanted to feel that in every way possible.

I broke from the kiss, leaving light nips on his lips as I did. Ransom's pupils were blown with lust and I knew mine looked the same.

"I want to touch you," I whispered.

"I want you to."

I unbuttoned his jeans and slid the zipper down. It might have been the best sound I've ever heard. The buzz of Ransom Fox's zipper coming down would be ingrained in my memory. I slipped a hand into his boxers and gripped him firmly. His back arched and I lowered my mouth to his again, jacking him ever so slowly. Pre-come paved the way for me to jerk him smoothly and I began to run my fingers around the rim of his cock on every upward stroke. He was writhing on the couch, his hips arching to meet my grip as I continued to kiss him.

My own cock was crying in my jeans and I rubbed against his thigh to get friction as I kept pumping his dick and devouring his mouth. I'd never been so turned on in my life. I wanted him to fuck me until I couldn't walk straight, but I knew we needed to take this slowly.

I knew exactly when Ransom was getting ready to blow. The head of his prick flared, a moan left his throat, and then his dick erupted all over my hand. I shot off in my jeans just watching him and I pumped him throughout, until he was swearing and panting. I pulled back from the kiss and Ransom licked his lips.

"Holy shit!"

"I know." I grinned, removing my hand from his dick. God help me, I couldn't help but lick some of his release off my hand.

"Fuck, that's hot." Ransom stared at me.

"You taste good."

"You're going to kill me," Ransom groaned.

"Did you like it?"

"Of course!" Ransom sat up a bit and kissed me lightly. "When can we do that again? Maybe do more?"

"Let's take this slowly, okay? I don't want this to only be about sex with us."

"Why would you think that?" Ransom's brows furrowed. "Is it because you've dated before and it was all about sex for them?"

"I haven't dated men, but I've had my share."

"Really? How?"

"When we're on location. I don't really go anywhere close to home. I wear a disguise too. When I was younger, I'd dated women and they only wanted me for two things — sex and the notoriety. That's why when I met Scarlett and she called me out, we came to an agreement."

"Aren't you lonely, though?"

"I've only wanted one man from the second I spotted him." I grinned and Ransom pulled me down into his arms. I rested my head on his chest and listened to his heartbeat. Was it possible to fall in love with someone from the second you spoke to them? I already had feelings for Ransom, but the more I got to know him, the stronger the feelings became.

"Um, I'm sticky," Ransom said, interrupting my

thoughts.

"Oh! Let's get cleaned up. I want to take you somewhere."

The sun was down and the lights of the city illuminated everything around us. Ransom stood next to me, suitably impressed. I loved it here, I really did. Whenever I needed time to myself to figure shit out, this is where I came.

"What is this place?" he asked.

"The observatory. I really like coming here when I just need to chill. I've gotten to know the staff, so they pretty much just let me hang out after hours."

"The view from up here is awesome." Ransom turned to me. "I could see why you wouldn't want to leave."

And that right there scared me to death, because for Ransom I'd leave. I'd leave it all behind if he was mine. I'd spent most of my life in front the camera. What would it be like to come home to Ransom every night?

"Sal?" Ransom searched my face. "It's okay, you know. I understand."

"You understand what?"

"How you can't leave here. I mean, California and New York are the biggest places to film movies. I know this is where you need to be."

"We have a lot to discover about each other, Ransom.

Let's take it easy." I took his hand. "Come on."

I led him over to the Astronomers monument and sundial. Ransom walked around taking it all in.

"There are six astronomers on this monument, all of them the most influential and important in history. At the top is the Armillary sphere and behind you is the sundial."

"You know a lot about this place, huh?"

"As I said, I spend a lot of time here."

"Ever bring one of your dates?" Ransom teased.

"No. I never have."

Ransom stopped walking and glanced over his shoulder at me. "Not once?"

"No. This place is very special to me, Ransom. I wanted you to see it because I think you're special too."

Ransom smiled at me and then discreetly looked around. My heart ached because I knew he wanted to hug me just then, or kiss me, but he was afraid someone would see us. This was the part I knew I was going to hate. Having to hide how I felt about Ransom Fox.

"I would love it if you came with me to Italy, too."

"I love Italy."

"My parents own a home in Praiano. I try to go there as often as I can."

"Where is that exactly?"

"It's a province of Salerno. There's a bar there that sits atop a hill and has a breathtaking view of the ocean.

There's also a path that runs around below. I love going there just as the sun is setting."

"I would love to see it." Ransom shot me a grin.

I stepped toward him and stopped when I heard a muffled 'ow' from somewhere. The next thing I knew the beefy bodyguard, Buster, walked out with a camera hanging around his neck.

"Buster?" Ransom said.

"Caught an asshole in the tree over there." Buster pointed behind him. "He's going to have one hell of a headache when he comes to. He was taking pictures of you guys."

"Fuck." Ransom hissed under his breath.

"I think you guys should head on out of here." Buster placed a hand at my lower back and pushed me forward.

"I can walk," I said wryly.

"Yes, well, do it faster." Buster ushered us all the way back to the car. He leaned in and addressed Ransom.

"I have his camera, but he really doesn't need it at this point. He'll tell someone he saw you two together and the paparazzi will be all over this. Lay low for a bit, eh? I'll do some damage control."

"Thanks, Buster."

We left and I drove home in silence. I didn't think Ransom wanted to talk about what was about to happen either. The paparazzi were like a dog with a bone when they got wind of something. I had a feeling things were about to hit the fan.

Chapter 9

"Are you sure this is a good idea?" I asked.

"I'm not going to sit around in my house with the blinds drawn, Ransom. I'm not going to be a prisoner in my own home."

Despite what Buster had told us the night before, Sal took me all over Hollywood the next day. I'd already seen his star, but he took a picture of the two of us standing next to it. We had Chinese food, walked all over, and laughed our asses off. We ran from the paparazzi at one point and ended up hiding behind a row of Dumpsters in an alley.

"God, this is so romantic," I whispered.

"I did promise you a good time."

My phone vibrated in my pocket and I pulled it out, swiping talk.

"Hello?"

"Mr. Fox? This is Dr. Lake. Paul is ready to go. We

need you to come in, sign some papers, and he's all yours."

"Thank you." I hung up and glanced at Sal. "Paul's ready to go."

"So, you are too." Sal touched my face lightly.

"Ahem."

We both glanced up to see Buster standing above us, arms crossed with a look of amusement on his lips.

"Yes?" I grinned.

"Coast is clear."

"You brought your bodyguard?" Sal asked, hiking up his brows.

"I don't bring Buster anywhere. He's just *there*," I clarified.

"If you guys make a run for it now, you should clear the mob that is coming up the street." Buster pulled out his phone and tapped at it. "I've got two guys up the road watching out."

I grabbed Sal's hand and wiggled my brows. "Ready?"

We ran out of the alley, both of us laughing hysterically. I almost tripped, but Sal caught me in time. We ran past a hoard of people and they all began shouting at us. Sal stopped and yanked me back.

"Are you crazy?" I asked.

"Nope. These people made me who I am. I can take some time out of my day to sign autographs. Plus, we can say you're visiting and I'm showing you around. Squash the rumors which are going to start. You up for it?"

I glanced over my shoulder to see Buster with two other men who made him look small. He nodded covertly and I swung my gaze back to Sal, hiking my shoulders up in a shrug.

"Let's do it."

I couldn't believe how much fun I was having. I kissed babies, hugged women and men and signed a ton of autographs. Sal and I took pictures with everyone there. It should have been scary, having that many people surround us, but they were all very nice. I answered a ton of questions about the next album and Sal answered questions about his next movie. When someone asked why we were together, Sal gave them the story we'd agreed on. People took it for what it was: two friends hanging out. Which was really all that we were doing.

I knew I wasn't ready for sex. Some touching and petting, sure, but not sex. I needed to get to know Salvatore Falcon. I decided on the last tour that I was done with sleeping around. My heart just wasn't in it anymore, and I wanted what Gareth had. We waved goodbye to all the people and I jumped into Sal's car. We waved as we went by and I noticed Buster climb into his own vehicle, following us.

"He's very stealthy," Sal observed.

"Buster? Yeah, he and two other security members came on during the European tour. Never been so happy to have them watching our backs."

We pulled into Sal's garage and he cut the engine. The garage door came down behind us and he pulled me into his arms. We kissed like we'd never see each other again.

I hoped that wasn't the case.

I loved the way he tasted, and the texture of his skin against mine. Every deliberate touch and swipe of tongue shattered me for anyone else. I was Sal's. We broke from the kiss, both of us a little disheveled and out of breath. Sal got out of his side and came around to mine, opening the door for me. I took his hand and then I was right back in his arms, kissing him and holding on as if I couldn't let go for fear of it all ending.

"I love the way you kiss. It's so sensual," Sal murmured across my lips.

"I can say the same about you. I feel like I'm drowning and I don't care."

"God, I'm going to hate it when you leave."

"We can still see each other, right? You've got time off?"

"Yes. I can come see you."

"Will you?" I asked hopefully.

"Yes, Ransom. I couldn't stay away even if I wanted

to."

My heart raced at those words. I wanted this to work. I just hoped it could.

I awoke to the sound of soft breathing behind me. Sal was spooned into my back and I grinned to myself. His hand was resting on my abdomen and I knew it belonged there. I'd never been so far gone for someone before. I'd always had a huge crush on Sal as a kid, but to actually be with him? Huge difference. I had to pick up Paul today and get back to Arizona. I hated the thought of leaving Sal, but we'd talked at length the previous night about not being away from each other for too long.

Sal stirred behind me and I rolled to my side, just staring at him. He had the most luscious lips I'd ever seen on a man and his eyelashes would make any woman jealous. They rested like silk on his copper-colored skin. His lips rose in a smile and I all but swooned.

"You're watching me sleep?" he asked, his eyes still closed.

"Can't help it. You know, I don't know if guys call other guys beautiful, but that's what you are."

"Really? Not sexy, or jaw-dropping handsome?"

"That too."

Sal's eyes fluttered open and fixed on mine. His eyes were arctic blue, but I could see grey and gold flecks, along with some light green.

"Your eyes change color?" I asked.

"Yours do too."

"They do?"

"Oh yeah." Sal brushed his fingers across my cheek and I shivered from his touch. "The first time I ever saw you, I wanted you so much it hurt."

I knew I was blushing. The guy I'd given my heart to at twelve was telling me he wanted me.

"I can wait, you know?" I said.

"For?"

"You, sex, a relationship. All of it."

Sal's smile slipped and I kicked myself. "I mean —"

"I know what you mean, Ransom. I want that too. I just don't know how we're going to make it work. But I'm going to give it everything I have. You mean a lot to me."

"You mean a lot to me too," I whispered.

"We'll take it one day at a time, all right? You're worth waiting for."

I kissed him then, just a soft peck on his lips but he pulled me in and held me against him. His warmth seeped into my whole body, heating me instantly. God, he smelled fantastic! I wanted to touch him just then, I wanted to give him what he had given me. I slid my hand over his bicep and down to his hip. I leaned in, kissing him as my hand traveled around to his ass.

"What are you doing?" Sal asked against my lips.

"I want to make you feel good."

"Ransom —"

"Just let me."

I brought my hand to the front of his pajama pants and traced my fingers alongside his morning erection. I played with the tip of his dick through the material before sliding a hand into his pants and gripping his thick shaft.

"Fuck," Sal rasped. "That feels so fucking good!"

I worked him slowly, letting my hand trail up and down his dick, squeezing a bit as I came up. I kissed him again as I began to work faster, his hips arching into my grip, sending his dick through my fingers. I was turned on just listening to him. My hips moved with my hand and Sal's finger's gripped my hair as I worked him. He was breathing heavily, his lips nipping at mine as I continued to jack him. The head of his prick swelled suddenly and then Sal was shouting through his orgasm, his seed splashing all over his chest. My dick erupted seconds later and I wrapped my leg around him, holding on to him while I basically shouted through my own release. We stayed there quietly, softly kissing as we came down.

"I can't believe I'm with you right now," Sal whispered.

"Me too. It's so damned surreal. I always wondered what it would be like to meet you and when I did, it was like I was the deer caught in the headlights. I couldn't think of a single word to say."

"You did fine. I had no idea you were into me."

"Really?" I asked suspiciously.

"Really. That's why I was so shocked when you kissed me back. I wanted you so much." Sal pulled me closer, running his nose through my hair. "We should shower."

We ended up making out in the shower until the water turned cold, then we sat on the couch with snacks and watched Sal's movies. I leaned back to check the time and frowned. I'd already packed what stuff I had and was dreading having to leave. Sal turned to face me and I saw the look in his eyes.

"I know," I said softly. "But we'll see each other again soon, right?" Sal kissed me and I knew that would have to tide me over.

Chapter 10

SAL

"So," I fidgeted. I really wanted to kiss him goodbye, even though we'd been kissing for hours. I didn't want him to go. I wanted him to stay with me.

"Yeah." Ransom carded a hand through his hair and grinned at me. "Soon, right?"

"Yes. Soon." I nodded.

Ransom got into his car and I almost gripped my chest. The pain was there, as though I was losing something.

"Ransom?"

"Yes?"

"I'm going to miss you."

"I know what you mean."

I waved as Ransom drove out of my driveway and right out of my life — at least for a few days. I had every intention of seeing him as soon as time would allow. I missed him already. I stepped back into the house and sifted through the mail. I had a few offers for movie roles again and I wasn't sure I was ready to take on another one. That would be weeks, maybe months away from Ransom and I wasn't ready to go there yet.

I wanted to be with Ransom at the airport when he left, but I knew I'd be tempted to kiss him. Fuck. Why couldn't I just be with him? I wanted to be, but the part of me that knew the backlash I'd get was hiding in the damn corner. It wasn't fair. I wanted to be with Ransom more than anything.

That stopped me cold.

More than my career?

I could see myself retiring. It wasn't as if I needed the money. I was well off, had invested money as well. I picked up the phone and chewed my lip. I dialed my mother and waited for her to answer. She did on the third ring.

"Salvatore!" she crooned into the phone. "When are you coming to visit?"

"I hope soon, Ma. I need to talk to you about something."

"You've found a man."

I stared at the phone, mouth open. "How did you know?" I said when I'd returned the phone to my ear.

"Your voice is full of excitement and happiness. Who is he?"

"Do you remember Ransom Fox?"

"Oh, yes! He is the singer of that ear-bleeding music you love so much."

"It's him, Ma. I just spent time with him and I think I'm falling for him. Is that even possible?"

"I have seen you swoon over this man for years, Salvatore. Yes, it is possible. I knew I loved your father from the moment he tripped me."

I laughed. The story with my mother and father was that he was so nervous about meeting her, he'd accidentally tripped her, and she'd fallen into a puddle of mud. He then got in with her and that, as they say, was that.

"What about my career? You know how it is out here, Ma."

"Things are changing. It may not be as bad as you think. Are you willing to give it all up for Ransom Fox?"

"Yes," I blurted immediately. Well, I guess I had my answer. When push came to shove, I'd leave it all behind for him.

"I'm so happy for you! I want you both to come visit, all right? Go get your man, Salvatore!"

"Ti amo, Ma."

"Voglio bene anch'io."

I hung up the phone feeling ten times better. I knew talking to my mom would clear my head about things. My father was just as understanding, thankfully. I texted

Ransom, telling him I already missed him and flopped down onto the couch with a smile. I read through some of the scripts anyway just to see what kind of roles they were. As always, I was the leading man in some steamy, sexy movie. I realized the day had gotten away from me somehow and it was now pushing eight at night. I checked my phone and noticed Ransom had sent me a kissy face. How cute was that? I sent one back and got comfortable on the couch. My whole body felt relaxed and I closed my eyes.

My phone rang, drawing me out of a deep sleep. I rolled over and fell off the couch. I searched for my phone and found it underneath on the floor, underneath the couch.

"Hello?"

"Sal, this is Dr. Holt. I need you to come in this morning."

"Does it have to be today?" I almost whined.

"Yes. Please come as soon as you can."

The line went dead and I stared at my phone, puzzled. What the hell could be so important? I got up and showered, dressed and was out the door in record time. I drove the back roads to avoid traffic and pulled into the parking lot by nine. I took the back entrance and found the doc's office. I knocked and got the 'come in' from the other side. As I stepped into the room, I felt a sense of dread come over me as Dr. Holt barely gave me a smile.

"What's up, doc?" I joked.

"Remember when you came in a couple weeks ago complaining of flu-like symptoms? You had a stomachache as well?"

"Yes, but that's gone now." Doc shook his head and I leaned forward. "What is it, doc? Don't hold back here."

"I ordered a full lab work up, just to cover all the bases. One of the things I tested you for was HIV, Sal. I didn't think anything of it and you said you were better, so I figured you were good. It wasn't until I came back from vacation and the tests results were here that I looked at them all. The test came back positive, Sal. Positive for HIV."

It felt as if the floor gave out beneath me. My chest constricted and I felt sick to my stomach. I couldn't pull in enough air and my face heated until I was sure it was on fire. I gripped the arms of the chair until my knuckles turned white. Somewhere, far away, the doctor was talking. I could see his lips moving, but the ringing in my ears was so loud I couldn't hear what he was saying.

"Sal! Breathe!"

Oh, fuck me. I was going to die. How was this

possible? The last time I'd been with anyone was a few months back, but he'd used protection. I *know* he did. I didn't know who he was and vice versa. HIV? How the fuck did I get HIV? My brain was working a mile a minute, but I couldn't concentrate on one thing at a time. I needed air. Oh, God, I couldn't breathe and the room was getting smaller and smaller. I was going to pass out.

Fuck.

I opened my eyes to find the doctor sitting beside me on the floor. My back was cold and I blinked up at him.

"I passed out," I said stupidly.

"Yes, you did. I know this is a lot to take in and we have a lot to do so bear with me, all right? I need to draw more blood and run a few additional tests and then we can go from there."

He kept talking, but the only thing I could hear was HIV.

I had HIV.

Oh, God. How? When? Why? I wanted answers and I needed them now. What the hell was I going to do? I couldn't have HIV. He had to be mistaken. OTHER people got HIV, not people like me. Who are those 'other' people, anyway?

"Sal, are you listening to me?"

I sat up and wrapped my arms around my knees. I tried to stop what I knew was about to come, but I couldn't.

Sure enough, I began to cry.

Arms came around me and I realized Dr. Holt was holding me, trying to soothe me. I couldn't stop crying. I'd been so damned careful! Eventually I stopped crying, wiped my eyes, and the doctor gave me some tissue.

"It's going to be all right, Sal. We will get this all sorted out," Dr. Holt told me.

He sent me off to the lab to get my blood drawn. I stared straight ahead as the nurse poked me. This wasn't happening. It was a nightmare that I would wake up from any minute. Right? Right? I couldn't have HIV. It just wasn't possible.

I was ushered back into the doc's office and he began going over things with me. What I'd need to do, who I'd need to see. It was overwhelming and I couldn't take it all in. I felt as though I was in some kind of fog and I couldn't see anything. I was so out of it, I didn't realize Scarlett was in the waiting room when I walked out. She rushed over to me and wrapped an arm around my waist.

"Sweetie! What's wrong? Doc called me and told me to get down here right away and pick you up!"

"Can we just go home? I just want to go home." I wanted to cry in the privacy of my own room. Shut the whole world away and pray I'd heard the doctor wrong — that the tests would come back and it was wrong. It was all so wrong.

Scarlett drove us home and I stared out the window, trying to make sense of everything. As soon as she pulled into the garage, I ran into the house and straight to the bathroom. I barely made it to the toilet and hurled the contents of my stomach into it. Scarlett was at my side in an instant, brushing my hair from my temple.

"Talk to me, Sal! What the hell happened?"

"Don't touch me!" I shouted. Scarlett slapped my head and I glared at her.

"Fuck you! What the hell is wrong with you?"

I busted out crying and Scarlett took me into her arms. "Please, tell me, Sal. You're scaring me," she whispered.

What would she think if she knew? Would she look at me in disgust? Would she even stay by my side? God, I didn't know what to do.

"Please. Talk to me, Sal. Whatever it is, we can deal with it."

I stood on shaky legs and held onto the sink for support. Scarlett's eyes were wet. She was crying too. I rinsed out my mouth and she walked with me to my room where I collapsed on the bed. I rolled to my side and started crying again. I couldn't stop. Scarlett got in bed with me and held me.

"I have HIV," I whispered.

Scarlett tensed for a brief second, then she held me

tighter.

"You're going to make it through this," she said. "It's not a death sentence, Sal. They have all kinds of new drug therapies these days."

"Ransom," I choked out.

"If he cares for you the way I know he does? He'll deal with this too."

"You're not... going to leave me?"

I felt her hand cuffing me on the back of my head. "What the fuck is wrong with you? Of course I'm not going to leave you!"

Scarlett began crying and we held each other.

"You're my best friend, Salvatore Falcon."

I think we both cried for hours. We were both sniveling messes by the time we actually got out of bed and headed to the kitchen to eat. Scarlett sat on the stool while I cooked us some food.

"So, what did the doc say? Does he know your T-cell count and viral load?"

I stared at her in disbelief. "How do you know so much?"

"Do you really think you're the first person to get HIV? I have a few other people I know who are positive, so I know quite a bit, Sal." She eyed me. "Are you going to tell Ransom?"

"I don't know if I can," I admitted. "Maybe this was

123

my wake-up call."

"Meaning?"

"Maybe I need to be alone."

"You need to be happy!"

"I'm gay, and according to the religious people, this is my punishment." Scarlett looked at me as if she couldn't believe she'd heard what I just said.

"You're seriously saying this, right now? All kinds of people get HIV! Gay or straight doesn't matter. HIV doesn't discriminate, Sal."

"I have a week to wait until I hear what the results are and I'm scared to death, Scarlett. I don't know if I can handle this."

"I'll be here every step of the way, Sal. You're not going to lose me, okay?" Scarlett took my hand and squeezed it.

"I'm scared," I whispered.

Scarlett stood and came around the island, taking me into her arms. I held her and the tears began again. My God, I couldn't stop crying. I was still hoping it was all a bad dream and I'd wake up in the morning and life would be normal. My phone buzzed and I picked it up, staring at the screen. It was Ransom.

I couldn't do this now. I just couldn't. I hit ignore and placed the phone on the counter. Scarlett looked down at the screen and then our eyes met.

"Don't push him away, Sal. You're going to need everyone around you."

"I can't, Scarlett. I just can't tell him. Not yet."

I knew she didn't approve, but I just couldn't do it. If I was going to tell Ransom, it would have to be face-to-face, and I couldn't even talk about it without crying. I didn't want him to feel like he had to stick around.

I felt like shit. Ransom called two more times and then he stopped calling. I had tried to start a text to him, but couldn't seem to push send. It had been forty-eight hours since I'd gotten the news and I still couldn't wrap my head around it. Tonight I was sitting on the back deck, watching waves pound into the surf. The moon was high and puffy clouds dotted the night sky.

I stared at my phone and began typing again. I knew Ransom was probably hurt and I also knew I needed to tell him something. I kept it short and sweet, then hit 'send.' I was going through all the stages at once it seemed. Crying, denying, anger. The worst part was the waiting — waiting to see how bad it was going to be. I would be on medication for the rest of my life.

I broke down again and sobbed. I hadn't cried this much in my entire life. Arms came around me and I let Scarlett hold me. My phone pinged and I looked down at the text. Ransom had texted me back.

"What did you say to him?" Scarlett asked.

"That I was going through something and to just give me time."

Scarlett picked up my phone and read the text. "I understand. If you need me, I'm here."

I cried again because I knew he might not be there for me once he found out I was sick — and that scared me more than anything else. Not just from Ransom, but from my coworkers, my agent, and directors.

"I think we need to go to a support group, hon," Scarlett murmured.

"I can't... they'll recognize me."

"I have one we can go to, okay? No one will say anything."

"How do you know?"

"Because they have just as much to lose." Scarlett took my hand and led me inside. "But for tonight? You are going to get some sleep."

"I don't know if I can. My mind starts working overtime and I can't fall asleep. I'm worried about what the tests will say, how sick I am."

"You can't change what you don't know, so please,

get in bed. I'll come with you. We'll watch a movie and take your mind off of it."

"I'm picking the movie."

"Not *Spaceballs*!" she narrowed her eyes to slits.

"*Spaceballs* it is."

I heard viral load almost undetectable and T-cell count high, which is apparently positive news. I also heard Truvada, two hundred milligrams, and Tivicay, fifty milligrams. After that, I didn't remember much. Dr. Holt was going over my medications list, which ones to take and when. I stared at the bottles of pills in my hand and knew I'd be taking them for the rest of my life. I moved in a fog after that. I went home, packed a bag, and left Scarlett a note. I didn't want to be around anyone.

I didn't know if I'd ever want to be around people again. I just knew I needed to go home to Italy. I was scared to death I'd somehow pass on HIV to Scarlett, or anyone else for that matter. I couldn't risk giving it to Ransom.

Going to Italy was my best bet. My parents' house had a villa off to the side and I could stay there while I tried to figure out what I was going to do. My grandfather was buried on the property and I knew I would be too. I called my lawyer as well, setting up provisions in case something happened to me. I left the house to Scarlett and everything else to Ransom. I waited for the email to come through and then gave my electronic signature. I took a look around the house, grabbed my bag and left.

I texted Ransom from the plane letting him know I would be flying into Flagstaff and the time I was arriving.

I needed to end it with him as soon as possible, because he deserved a life and I couldn't give it to him.

Chapter 11

I was so excited! I didn't know what had happened to Sal, but his cryptic text a little less than a week ago had scared me. I thought things had been going well when I left, and then he'd texted and said he was dealing with something. I tried so hard not to be a little bitch about it, but when he'd pretty much cut me off it really hurt. The airport was practically empty, no big surprise there. Flagstaff Pulliam Airport was small and only a few flights came in and out each day. I watched as the jet stopped and the stairs unfolded. Sal walked down them, across the tarmac and came through the door. I rushed to him and flung my arms around his neck.

"God! I missed you!"

Sal's arms didn't come around me and he stiffened in my embrace. I pulled back a bit and tried to meet his gaze, but he wouldn't meet mine.

"Sal? What is it?"

"This isn't going to work, Ransom."

"What do you mean?" I asked, my stomach plummeting.

"We're too different. We live in two different states."

"Wait, we can get around the different states. Why are we so different? We actually have a lot in common, Sal."

I could see him wrestling with something and I reached a hand out only to have him back away from me.

"Don't touch me!"

I recoiled at his harsh words and stepped back. "Why are you acting like this? I thought… well, I thought we were starting something here."

"It's not going to happen, Ransom. I'm not going to give up my career for you."

"I never asked you to! I didn't say you had to come out, either. We can make this work. I think we're worth it."

"I don't," Sal snapped.

I knew I was about to cry. God help me, I never cried, but that was about to change. I clasped my hands together and closed my eyes.

"So you're saying you used me all this time? You wanted to cop a feel and kiss me and that's it?"

"I'm done, Ransom. Go home." Sal turned on his heel and walked away.

"You're lying!" I shouted. It reverberated through the whole airport and Sal stopped. "Tell me the truth!"

"I can't," he said softly, and then walked through the doors.

I watched him getting further and further away, my heart aching with every foot he put between us. What the hell had just happened? Why was Sal walking away from me? We were good together; I knew it and so did he. What the fuck had happened for Sal to walk away from me? I didn't push him into anything. I bit my lip and got into my car, trying to hold back what I knew was going to be a hell of a crying jag.

I made it to the hospital and ducked by all the people, trying to remain unnoticed as I headed for Paul's room. I opened the door and shut it quickly behind me.

"Hey! Perfect timing. I'm ready to — Ransom? What's wrong?"

And that's when I lost it. I crumpled to the floor and began an all-out sob-fest. Paul rushed to my side and gathered me into his arms. I held him tightly, unleashing all of my anger and sadness into his shirt.

"What the fuck did he do?" Paul practically growled. "Did he hurt you?"

"He… he…" I hiccupped and broke into another fit of uncontrollable sobbing.

"I'm here," Paul murmured into my hair. "I'm right here. Just let it out."

I couldn't stop crying. Maybe it made me a little bitch but I couldn't seem to care just then. The guy I'd fantasized about my whole life had just thrown me away without even telling me why. I couldn't breathe. I was so full of snot and Paul removed his shirt, holding it up to my nose.

"Blow," he instructed.

"I'm not blowing my nose into your shirt," I sniffled.

"Fine. Hang on."

Paul got up and I wiped my eyes again. He came back with some tissue and I blew my nose. He held me again and I buried my face in his neck.

"Tell me, Ransom," he said quietly.

So I did. I could tell Paul was getting angry as I relived the entire week with Sal to him. He didn't say anything, just listened and I'd never been more grateful to have him.

"Come on." Paul stood and offered me his hand.

"Where are we going?"

"Out."

I signed Paul out and we jumped into my car. Paul got behind the wheel and when I opened my mouth to protest he shot me a look that sent me inching into the passenger's seat. We drove out of the parking lot and into town. Paul took a side road and then I knew where we were going. I stared out the window. Snow had begun to fall. Huge flakes whirled around us as we drove out to our favorite camping spot. Once Paul parked the car, he got out and walked to the ridge. I followed, hands stuffed into my pockets.

"Do you see that?" Paul pointed toward the red rock of Sedona.

"Seems so far away," I murmured.

"But it's not. Everything is just within your reach. You just have to grab it." Paul turned to look at me. "I don't know what happened to make Sal do what he did, but you are not going to sit here and wallow in it. Got it? I know that man is in love with you."

"How do you know?"

"Because I remember when I used to look at you that way."

"Paul —"

"Just let me finish, will ya? The minute I met Sal, I knew he was a goner for you. He knew it too. I called him out right there and then. I don't know what happened, but I'd bet my left nut it's something you can change."

I searched Paul's eyes. "You think so?"

"Ransom," Paul sighed. "Anyone would be an idiot to walk away from you. You're the kindest person I know, besides Gareth. You could have sent me to jail, not put me in a hospital to help me. Who the fuck does that? I pulled a gun on your brother!"

"But —"

"No! Stop making excuse for me! Don't get me wrong. I love you guys, but you're so damned forgiving. You should have let me rot in a damn cell for what I did."

"We're not going to argue about this again!" I shouted. "You didn't need jail, you needed help! I'm not turning my back on family, dammit!"

Paul grinned and I cocked a brow. "What?"

"There's my fierce warrior. Now apply that to the jackass who just hurt you." Paul took my hand.

"I'll think about it. Can we go now? I'm fucking freezing!"

"Yeah, but I'm getting a Wicked Arizona coffee on my way back to Loonieville."

I drove us back and we stopped at the coffee shop. I felt like I was on autopilot. I was driving and talking but not really paying attention to anything. I pulled into the parking lot and walked with Paul back to his room. I sat down on his bed and stared straight ahead. I felt completely empty inside.

"Hey." Paul took a seat next to me. "I know this is hard on you, but we're going to get you back with Sal, okay?"

"Thank you for being here, Paul." I hugged him.

"Hey, we're family, right?"

"Yeah, we are."

I was on a flight to Los Angeles the next day. I had no clue where Sal had gone, but he'd made it a point to see me in person and end it, so I was going to see him in person and restart it. Something had to have happened for him to react this way. Did the media call him out? Did they start rumors about him being gay? I could fix it. I knew I could.

I pulled up to Sal's house and hit the intercom.

"Ransom?" Scarlett's voice floated out over the drive.

"Can you let me in?"

The gate opened and I drove around to the front of the house. Scarlett came out and stood just outside the front door. I exited the car and strode right up to her.

"Where is he?" I asked.

"I don't know." She shook her head.

I pushed past her into the house and glanced around. "Sal! Where are you?"

"He's not here, Ransom." Scarlett shut the door and

strode into the kitchen.

"Where is he?"

"I told you. I don't know. He said he needed to be alone even though I told him he shouldn't be."

"What the hell happened, Scarlett? Why did he fly all the way out to Flagstaff just to tell me it was over?"

"He ended it with you?" Scarlett shook her head, cursing under her breath. "That man is so damned stubborn!"

"What happened, Scarlett? Tell me the truth!"

"I can't tell you." Scarlett lifted her eyes to mine.

"He told you, but couldn't tell me?"

"It's not something I'm at liberty to share."

"Dammit, Scarlett! I need to know why he just dumped me. We were... I mean, things were going well between us."

"Look, I'm sorry, but it really isn't my place to tell you."

"I know he felt something for me, Scarlett. This wasn't one-sided!"

Scarlett paced the kitchen and then her head snapped up to me. "What would be the one thing a gay actor in Hollywood wouldn't want made known besides the fact he's gay?"

"He's got a love child?"

Scarlett narrowed her eyes at me. I wracked my brain

trying to think about what she'd said. What would be the one thing someone wouldn't want getting out? A gay person wouldn't want anyone to know? I paced the living room and bit my lip in concentration. An idea popped into my head and I turned to see Scarlett's face. It looked like she'd been crying and then it all slammed into me at once.

"HIV?" I guessed quietly.

Scarlett nodded.

"Oh, God," I whispered.

"He left me a note and his lawyer called me. He's acting as if he's going to die, drawing up a will and everything. Does this change how you feel about him?"

I stared at her and pulled my keys out of my back pocket. "You don't know me at all, do you?" I walked to the front door and Scarlett gripped my bicep.

"Where are you going?"

"Where do you think? If you hear from him, find out where he is."

I walked out and practically ran to my car. Sal thought he was going to get rid of me that easily? Oh, he had another think coming.

Chapter 12

Gareth picked me up from the airport in Flagstaff. I had a lot to do and one of my first stops was with my doctor. I needed to know everything about being with Sal and what to do to make that happen. Gareth didn't say anything as I threw my bag in the backseat and slammed the door.

I looked out the window as Gareth drove me home. I couldn't believe it. My relationship with Sal was over before it even began. I was willing to do anything it took to be with him.

"Ransom?"

"What?" I snapped.

"I'm sorry," Gareth barely whispered.

I turned to look at my little brother. He looked sad for me. I took his hand and he shot a look at me sideways. No matter what, I still had the band and my little brother.

"I'm sorry I snapped at you. I'm just at a loss right now."

"You know what you need?" he waggled his brows.

I narrowed my eyes. "No."

"Oh yeah!" Gareth snickered and pushed a button on his stereo.

The next thing I knew, Vanilla Ice's *Ice, Ice, Baby* was flowing out of the speakers. Despite my anger and sadness, I began to laugh. Gareth and I had some weird music we used to unwind and laugh at life. We both began to sing at the top of our lungs, windows open and the cool mountain air brushing across our faces.

No matter what was going on in my life, no matter how fucked up it got, I knew I could rely on my little brother to make me feel better.

And I really felt like shit.

I'd given Sal something I'd never given anyone else — my heart.

I had cried in the bathroom of the plane and the bathroom at the airport. I was over the crying. Gareth glanced over at me with a grin.

"You're going to fight, aren't you?" he asked.

"Fuck, yes."

"Good. Now can you tell me what this is all about?"

"You're sworn to secrecy." I pointed at him.

"And I've been untrustworthy when?" Gareth slid me

a look.

So I told him. Gareth didn't interrupt me, he just listened. When I was done, he nodded and glanced at me.

"We need to go to the clinic."

"Yes, we do. I need to know what I'm in for."

"Not just that. Do you remember when we sat in on the support group for HIV patients? The spouses felt as though they were being abandoned, as if their positive partner was pulling away. That's what Sal is doing — alienating everyone from his life."

"Well, I'm not going to let him do it to me."

"It's not going to be easy, Ransom. If you just want Sal for his looks —"

"Are you fucking kidding me right now? Of course it's not all about how he looks!" Gareth chuckled and I glared at him. "Fuck off."

"I just needed to hear you say it, bro."

We pulled back into town and Gareth drove me to the clinic. We were welcomed with smiles and hugs and asked the director when the next HIV support group would be meeting. Once we got all the info, I went and saw the doctor on call. I sat down and explained the situation to him.

"Are you sure this is what you want, Ransom?" he asked. "Relationships are hard enough as it is. You add in this and it becomes even harder."

"I've never run from a fight in my life, doc. I'm not

about to start."

"All right. I'm going to start you on Tivicay. The likelihood of you contracting the disease will be much lower, but you are still going to have to practice safe sex to be as safe as possible."

"We haven't gotten that far, anyway."

"I'm going to run an HIV test on you nonetheless."

"Fine by me."

Once I'd gotten my meds, Gareth and I headed out to my house. We called the guys and they were meeting us. I knew I could trust them all with this, and I had every intention of having Sal in my life for the long haul. I filled Gareth in on everything that had happened while I was in L.A. and how Paul was adjusting to the new facility.

"Dude, you met Jasper Jamison?" Gareth said slowly. "Is he cool?"

"He's awesome — and get this — he knew who I was!"

"Holy shit!"

"I know, right? Sal was so nice to blow off all the other parties and take me to Jasper's. Although, according to Jasper, Sal attends a lot of his parties."

"So, how are you really?" Gareth sat down and held a hand out to me.

"I'm hurt, but I know I can get him back. He's not

going to just blow me off because he has HIV."

The front door to my place opened and Rebel strode in with Grandpa. At least he had clothes on.

"Hey, Grandpa!" I walked over to him and hugged him.

"Ransom?"

"Yes, Grandpa, it's me."

"Did you get taller?"

I shot a look at Rebel, who merely shrugged. Grandpa was in the beginning stage of Alzheimer's, so his memories were hit and miss when it came to the guys.

"Nope. Still six foot." I grinned.

"Where is the munchkin?" Grandpa eyed the room.

Gareth sighed and walked over to us. "I'm right here."

I took Rebel aside while Grandpa fussed over Gareth. He looked tired, like he hadn't gotten any sleep.

"What happened to you?" I asked.

"Been up watching him. Another nurse just quit." Rebel ran both hands down his face. "I don't know what to do. I don't want to put him in a home for good. He already goes to the nursing home all week for a few hours to visit friends. I'm running out of options on home-care nurses."

"We'll figure something out, okay? Who is watching him when he's not at the nursing home?"

"Stan, and I feel bad about it, but Grandpa loves

him." Rebel searched my eyes. "What happened in L.A.?"

"Let's wait for the other guys to show up, okay?"

"Sure." Rebel nodded.

One by one, my family arrived. I smiled as Jinx walked in with Jayden, his boyfriend. Harley was next with Achilles, and Harley looked so much better. His semi-alienated parents were starting to come around, and I think Achilles had a lot to do with it. Harley hadn't forgiven them as of yet, but he was seeing them more often. The guys were settling into the couch when there was a knock on the door. I furrowed my brows and crossed the room to it. Stan Jackson stood, unsure, on my steps. He was the band's manager now.

"Um, hey." He half-waved. "Gareth told me to come?"

"Why are you knocking?" I asked.

"Well… I just… I mean —"

"Stan, you're part of this family now. Get in here."

"I've brought Paul with me. Gareth asked me to."

"Come on in."

Stan blushed a bit, but strode into the room, taking a seat next to Grandpa. Paul came in and hugged me, taking a seat as well. The guys all clapped him on the back and he and Achilles shook hands. I arched a brow and sighed.

"Buster?"

"Yes?" Buster poked his head out of the kitchen.

"Could you guys join us?"

"We weren't sure if you wanted us out there." Buster entered with Hammer and Axel.

"Of course, I do. What I am about to say does not leave this room. We're all family so I expect to keep this hush-hush. Is that clear?"

"Yes." They all nodded and said at once.

"I began a relationship with Sal Falco while I was in L.A. —"

"I knew it!" Jinx shouted.

"Shut up." I pointed at him. "You guys were right. Scarlett is his beard. There was an earthquake and I freaked out. Sal kissed me to calm me down and it went from there. We were really happy." I bit my lip and fought back the tears I knew were going to start. "Something happened after I left and Sal flew into Flagstaff and ended things with me."

"What happened?" Harley asked.

I glanced at Gareth and he nodded. "Sal found out he has HIV."

"Lord! I thought you were going to say he had some kind of cancer or something, boy!" Grandpa blurted. "HIV is manageable. Damn, Betty down at the nursing home has had HIV for years."

"What?" my mouth dropped open.

"Oh, yeah. See, old people think they are safe from

shit like that, so they don't bother to use protection. So now you've got some ninety-year-old man with elephantiasis of the nuts and then he's pissing fire and eventually his dick falls off. Now me? I always wrap my dick —"

"Grandpa." Rebel slapped a hand over his grandpa's mouth.

"*Anyway*, Sal thought he was just going to end things with me and go off on his own. I'm not going to let it happen."

"We can find him," Axel spoke up.

"I was counting on it." I winked.

"The guys and I will get started right away." Axel nodded to Achilles and he stood, dropping a kiss on Harley's lips as he moved with the other bodyguards back into the kitchen.

I stood, staring at my friends. They were all smiling and I lifted a brow.

"What?" I asked.

"I'm damn proud of you, Ransom." Grandpa stood and pulled me into his arms. "Not everyone can deal with this kind of news the way you have."

"I've been to enough HIV support groups to know what comes next, Grandpa. I know it's not going to be easy."

Grandpa pulled back a bit and searched my features. "He's going to push you away."

"He already has, and I'm not going to let him keep doing it."

"That's my boy!" Grandpa turned to Rebel and Stan. "Which one of you is going to take me to bingo?"

"Grandpa, you don't play bingo." Stan sighed.

"Oh, that's right. I yell that as I'm coming." Grandpa waggled his brows.

"Oh, hell." Stan covered his face with his hands.

"Grandpa. You need Jesus." I laughed.

"All of you need to start attending church," Grandpa said seriously. "I don't want you in hell with me."

"Grandpa." Rebel stood and took his hand. "Let me take you to the nursing home. I hear it's meatloaf day."

"I've got the meat right here." Grandpa grabbed his junk.

The guys cracked up and Grandpa winked at me. I knew what he was doing — old man or not, he was trying to liven the mood, and I loved him for it.

Rebel left with Grandpa and I sat on the couch next to Stan and Jayden. Jinx and Harley sat on the arms of the couch and Gareth sat on the floor in front of me. The bodyguards were busy in the kitchen and I noticed Jayden's furrowed brows.

"What is it, Jayden?"

"Well, I could ask Sebastian about Sal. They *are* best friends."

"We'll do that if the guys can't pinpoint him. Thanks for bringing it up, though. How are you? Recovering from the tour?"

"Yes. Jinx has been making sure I sleep and eat right." Jayden glanced over at Jinx with a grin.

"Yeah? How are the other guys?" I asked.

"Evander went to Washington State for a bit, not sure about the twins. I think they may have gone home to Greece to hang out. When we come off a tour, we kind of scatter. I mean, we keep in touch but we do our own thing."

"Yeah, that really doesn't happen with us," Harley cut in. "We hang out together all the time. It's always been that way, though, since we were kids. I think the longer you guys are together, the more you'll gravitate towards each other after the tours."

I glanced over to see Paul looking a bit pale. I moved to him and crouched in front of him. "Hey, what's wrong?"

"I… I don't know. I'm feeling anxious again."

"You've been out of the hospital a lot lately, maybe that's why?"

"I think it is," Paul admitted softly.

"I can take you back?"

"I've got it, Ransom," Buster said, walking into the room. "It *is* too much. You're used to being in your room or out in the courtyard. Not surrounded by people in a small environment."

147

"Okay, doc," Paul snorted.

"I'll make sure he gets back." Buster nodded to me.

"All right." I hugged Paul. "Thank you," I murmured into his ear.

"Always."

Chapter 13

I stared out across the water as fishing boats headed back to shore. The sun was making its descent and I think it was the most beautiful sight I'd ever seen. I was taking notice of things now — the rain and wind on my skin, the smell of the ocean and the blueness of the sky. I'd noticed them before, but now it was in more vivid detail. I wanted to remember it all, see it in my mind's eye whenever I needed it.

I was home, in Italy, avoiding my parents. I'd gone straight to the villa, ignoring their pleas to speak to me. God knew I needed to tell them what was going on, but I needed some time to think about it all and what it meant. I would never be able to be with someone intimately again. I wouldn't make another movie either. No one would want to work with someone who was HIV positive.

I was finished in Hollywood.

I leaned back, letting the descending sun warm my face. My doctor told me HIV wasn't a death sentence, but why did I still feel as if it was? Any little cold I got from now on could possibly kill me. How was that living? Afraid to go out, to get sick, to make love. I wiped at my eyes and sniffled. Again with the damn crying. I couldn't seem to stop, and the worst part of it all was I missed Ransom terribly.

"Well, look at you."

I started and jumped to my feet. Sebastian was behind me, one hand raised to shield his eyes. "You look like hell, my friend."

"What are you doing here?"

"Did you really think your parents wouldn't have called me the moment you refused to speak to them? They have me on speed dial, love. Now tell me what is going on."

"I can't." I shook my head. I didn't want to lose Sebastian either. He'd been my friend for longer than I could remember.

"Are you dying?" he asked.

My head snapped up and our eyes met. His face changed immediately and he strode over to me with purpose. "Tell me now! We can fix this! We'll go to Switzerland, they've gone way above and beyond what the U.S. has."

"I can't," I whispered.

"Dammit, Salvatore! You had better come clean with me right now!" Sebastian thundered.

"Promise you won't leave me."

"What? Come on —"

"Promise!" I shouted.

"Of course I promise not to leave you, you nitwit! Now tell me what I can do to help you."

"I have HIV," I said quietly.

Sebastian sighed and held his head. "Jesus! You scared the shit out of me! I thought you were dying!"

"Didn't you hear me? I have HIV," I said it more slowly.

"I'm not deaf. Have they begun your medication regimen? What are your numbers?"

I stared at him openmouthed. What was with everyone? Scarlett knew about the medication and now it seemed Sebastian did too. I told him what the doctor had prescribed for me and he nodded, staring at me.

"A little over 1,200 and my CD-4 was high at 1,365."

"Well, you've begun taking it, right? Do you feel sick at all?"

"I feel fine," I admitted.

"Then why are you acting like you've got one foot in the grave? Jesus, Sal. People live long, healthy lives with HIV — even AIDS. What makes you think you're so damned special that it's going to kill you in a month?"

"I'm scared, Sebastian," I whispered. "I'm so fucking scared!"

"Then you hang onto those you love. We're all here to help you; you don't go off on your own to deal with it. Tell me what else has got your knickers in a twist."

"Ransom Fox."

"What? He gave it to you?!"

"No! Ransom didn't give me HIV. Why would you even think that?"

"He's a rock star, sleeping around every night. Of course, I would think that. Especially knowing your sexual encounters can be counted on one hand. So, he was keeping you busy. No wonder I haven't heard from you."

"I'm sorry. I meant to call, but then I got so busy trying to show him around town and spend as much time with him as I could, and now this."

"Where is Ransom? Did he not take the news well?"

I bit my lip and fidgeted.

"Oh, Christ! You didn't tell him?"

"I couldn't! I couldn't handle seeing how he would look at me. So I stopped in Flagstaff before I came here and ended it."

"You're a wanker."

"Excuse me?"

"You didn't even give the bloke a chance! Ransom Fox doesn't strike me as the type of man to walk away from something like this. Have you never seen Ransom and his band at the HIV/AIDS events?"

"W-What?" I stammered.

"I thought you knew everything about Ransom Fox?" Sebastian lifted a brow.

"I knew he gave money to them."

"Yes, well, he attends as well and he hugs everyone. Doesn't strike me as the type of man to shy away. Don't you agree?"

I turned my back to Sebastian and eyed the sun as it kissed the water. "I can't, Sebastian — at least not yet."

"When, then? After you've broken his heart into a million pieces? Though I'm sure you've done that already."

"I can't think about that right now."

"Oh, yes. You want to wallow, right? Well, I'm not going to let you. Now, let's go back to the villa and have a drink."

"I shouldn't. Not on my meds."

"Then I will." Sebastian extended a hand to me and I took it. He pulled me into a hug and I closed my eyes. "I am always here for you, Salvatore. You've been there for me; now let me be here for you. We'll tell your parents."

I was nervous as we pulled up in front of my parent's house. I knew they loved me; they'd loved me through every part of my life thus far. Sebastian held my hand firmly as we entered the house. Large trees were on all four corners of the sunken living room; they went through the roof and were surround by glass so when it rained, it rained indoors. It was beautiful to watch and it was actually the one thing that had calmed me down as a child.

My mother rounded the corner and stopped, staring from me to Sebastian.

"That doesn't look like Ransom Fox," she said.

"Hello, Aria. How are you?" Sebastian said smoothly as he left my side to embrace my mother.

"I am well, Sebastian. I'm glad you called." She eyed me closely. "Salvatore, what is wrong? Why did you not come to see us when you arrived? You've holed yourself up in the villa."

Sebastian nodded to me and I sighed. "Is Dad around?"

"He is." She nodded.

"Can I tell you together? I don't want to repeat myself."

"Yes. I will go get him. Meet us in the kitchen."

"Good, I'm getting some wine." Sebastian walked ahead of me. He stopped and glanced over his shoulder at me. "Move it, Salvatore."

I followed Sebastian into the kitchen and sat at the table. He brought me a glass of water and eyed the time.

"Have you taken your medication today?"

"Yes."

"Good, I don't want you thinking you can skip a day because you feel fine."

"I'm not going to skip any of them, okay?" I exhaled in frustration.

My father walked in and my mother followed him in. His hair was salt and pepper now and I thought back to what Scarlett had said a few years back. Women age, men become more distinguished. My mother was still beautiful, however. Even in her seventies, she looked fifty. My father sat down and my mother took the seat across from his. Sebastian was standing at the counter, pouring wine for them.

"So, Salvatore," my father began. "Why have you been hiding from us?"

"I went to the doctor a while back. I wasn't feeling well and thought I had the flu or something." I lifted my eyes to Sebastian's and he nodded for me to continue. "Well, it turns out I have HIV."

The room got so quiet I thought they'd stopped breathing, and then my mother began to cry. I wanted to go to her, but then I didn't know if I wanted to touch her.

"Mom," I began.

"No." She lifted a hand. "I am all right. I'm just worried about you. I know you will be taking medication for the rest of your life now. I am worried about the talk which will begin, the people who will shun you."

"Yes, the stupid ones," my father snapped. "You do not need them, Salvatore. Anyone who treats you differently was not your friend to begin with. Hollywood is filled with backstabbing people. It is why your mother and I left."

"Hey!" Sebastian balked.

"Not you, Sebastian," my father said with a small smile. "*You* are family."

My mother's brows furrowed and her eyes snapped to mine. "Ransom? Was he the one —"

"No, Ransom didn't give it to me. In fact, I'm scared to death I gave it to him. I ended things with him because I don't think he should have to deal with the backlash ahead."

"Bullshit!" Sebastian roared. "You ended things with him because you're scared! You didn't even give him the chance to make his own decision. You took that away from him and if I know Ransom Fox, he's going to be pissed as hell that you did this."

"Do not push those who love you away, Salvatore. You need everyone around you. Do you understand me?" My mother rose from the table and came around to me, wrapping her arms around me. I stiffened and tried to pull out of her embrace. "Stop it! You are not going to give me HIV by hugging me, Salvatore. Haven't you read up on everything?"

I hated to admit it, but I hadn't. I'd been so freaked out I didn't bother to do any research on it. I shook my head and my mother kissed my cheek. It felt wonderful to have her arms around me, to feel her skin on mine. I didn't feel like such a leper for a few seconds.

"I am glad you told us, Salvatore." My father stood as well and came around to me. My mother let go of me and my father pulled me up from the chair, wrapping his arms around me. God, for the thousandth time I was going to cry. I swallowed hard, fighting back the tears and my mother joined in the hug and then Sebastian did as well. The four of us stood there and finally my father broke the embrace.

"Let us get you educated, Salvatore. The one thing I want you to remember is you're not going to infect anyone just by holding their hand or hugging them. Did you have sexual relations with Ransom?"

"Dad!" I exclaimed, my face turning beet red. "No. I mean we didn't have anal sex." I couldn't believe I was talking about gay sex with my parents. I knew they were fine with me being gay but talking about it? Weird.

"Come on." My father pulled me into the living room and booted up his laptop.

We all sat around reading up on HIV. My mother left

at one point to make dinner, but then we were all eating around the laptop still reading articles. I knew I had a long way to go, but some of the information actually helped ease my mind a bit. I didn't know if I could be with anyone intimately for a long time, though. That part still scared me.

We cleaned the kitchen and my parents said goodnight to me and Sebastian. The two of us sat on the veranda, Sebastian with a glass of wine and me with water. The stars seemed brighter than usual and the constellations were in full view.

"When are you going to call him?" Sebastian's voice broke through my thoughts.

"I don't know, Sebastian. Wouldn't he be better off this way?"

"No, and neither would you."

I closed my eyes and inhaled slowly. Wouldn't I rather have Ransom in my life than not at all? Of course I would, but to subject him to the life I was going to have to live wasn't fair to him. I missed him. The touch of his hand, the warmth of his lips, I missed it all.

"Don't be stupid, Sal," Sebastian warned.

"I'll think about it in the morning. I'm tired. Are you staying?"

"Of course. I'm not leaving you. I also think you should call Scarlett and let her know you're okay."

Was I? I had no idea where to go from here. All the

things I'd wanted in life felt superficial now. Being famous and having money could only go so far. Money couldn't cure my HIV; being famous wouldn't do it either.

"You have many more years ahead of you, Sal. Don't waste your life alone."

Sebastian stood and bent, placing a kiss on the top of my head. He walked back into the house and I curled up on the lounger. My head hurt and my muscles ached, probably because I hadn't been able to relax in days. I lifted off the chair and headed to my old room in the house. I sat on the bed and just stared at the wall. There was a soft knock and the door opened a crack. My mother poked her head in.

"You are still awake?" I nodded and she came in, closing the door behind her. "Get in bed, Salvatore."

I did as she asked and she got in on the other side. I rolled to my side and my mom began running her fingers through my hair. As a child, if I were worried or scared, she would do this for me.

"It will be all right, Salvatore," she whispered.

God, how I wanted it to all be okay. To have Ransom at my side and live a long happy life.

"You will see."

I called Scarlett when I knew she'd be home. She answered on the second ring already screaming into the phone. I waited for her to take a breath before interrupting.

"I'm fine, and I'm sorry I left the way I did, Scarlett."

"I don't want the house you asshole! I want you! Stop acting like you're dying, dammit!"

"Are you done?"

"Maybe. I don't know. Are you coming home?"

"Not any time soon. You're welcome to join me here at my parents'."

"I'll come out as soon as I can. Please tell me you've been in touch with Ransom?"

"I haven't, and before you yell at me, I was planning on it."

"He knows," she whispered.

"What do you mean he knows? Did you tell him?"

"Not directly, I gave him one clue and he figured it out. I'm sorry, Sal but I just couldn't let you let him go. He's good for you."

"Was he... I mean, how did he take it?"

"I asked him if it changed how he felt about you. He said that I didn't know him at all. He cares Sal, and you really should call him."

I had so much other stuff to think about; I wanted to get my ducks in a row before I called Ransom. I needed to figure out where I was going from here. If Ransom was willing to stand by my side, I knew I could go through anything.

"I will, Scarlett. I promise. See you soon?"

"Yes, and Sal?"

"Yes?"

"I love you."

"Love you too, Scarlett."

Chapter 14

I paced my living room and Gareth watched me. I was starting to worry the guys wouldn't be able to find Sal. I missed him so much and the thought of him having to deal with his diagnosis by himself was seriously freaking me out. I wanted to hold him, to reassure him I wouldn't leave him and I'd be there through it all. Gareth coughed lightly and I stopped pacing.

"What?"

"We have to go. Support group meeting?" Gareth pointed to his watch.

"Okay."

Gareth drove, as I was in no shape to concentrate. I was worried shitless and couldn't seem to stop fidgeting. By the time we arrived, most of the group had gathered in a circle. I took one of the chairs and Gareth sat beside me. I listened to all the stories and my heart ached. It wasn't fair.

HIV and the stigma attached to it — it wasn't right. One of the kids spoke up and I was amazed at how well he was dealing with his diagnosis. He informed the group he'd been HIV positive for four years and in that time, he'd been called every name in the book. His girlfriend had given it to him and they were still together.

"Can I ask something?" I raised a hand.

"Sure."

"When you were first diagnosed, did you run away?"

A lot of the heads bobbed and I shook my head. It seemed like a common theme and Sal had just done the same thing.

"It's like, you want to be as far away from people as you can get," the kid spoke up. "We went through a lot of counseling, but we made it out the other side. Life is precious and HIV is not a death sentence. Did things change? Yeah, they sure did. For the better. We stop now, you know? Smell the rain, play in the snow, watch the sun rise and set. I want to spend every single day seeing the things I didn't bother to notice before. It's a second chance at a life you didn't realize you weren't living."

"Thank you." I took his hand with a smile.

"The thing is, as the negative partner, you'll be dealing with a lot. Your partner is going to pull away, you'll feel abandoned at times, but you have to reinforce that love every single day." He leaned in and grinned. "Kick ass if you know what I mean."

"I do." I nodded.

After another hour, the meeting broke up and everyone headed for the coffee machine. I stood at the window, watching snow float down in huge flakes. Gareth was beside me in an instant and he threaded our fingers together. I squeezed his hand and got a squeeze back. I smiled at our reflections in the window. I was ready to be with Sal, whether he liked it or not.

I sat in the passenger seat of the car and thought of all the things in my life that would need to change and I didn't care. Wasn't that what Gareth and I had always said? When you love someone, you take them with the good and the bad. I'd fallen in love with Sal and now I wanted my life to start again, with him in it. I glanced over at Gareth and he shot me a look. He pulled the car over and cut the engine.

"Why are we stopping?" I asked.

"I want you to go all out for Sal. Understood?"

"What are you talking about? I'm going to get him and bring him home."

"If he wants to stay in California, you're going to stay with him."

"What? No, I can't do that. My life is here with you —"

"Ransom, you have to let go," Gareth said softly. "I know you feel responsible for me, but I'm not the tiny, sick baby in the incubator anymore. I'm a grown man with a husband who will kill anyone who tries to hurt me. I love you, more than I can express, but you have to let me go, Ransom." Gareth took my hand. "You've been there for me through everything. Let me be there for you, okay? You deserve a life with the man you love. I'm going to be fine."

I took a good, long look at my brother. God, he'd come so far. He was a man and I needed to remember that. Part of me would always want to hold him close, shelter him from the bad, but Axel had his back now. I smiled and squeezed his hand.

"Okay, Gareth. Whatever you want."

We arrived at my house to find Axel's car in the driveway. I barely waited for Gareth to pull in before I jumped out and ran. They had to have known where Sal had run off to by now. When I came through the door, Axel turned to me with a grin.

"You found him?"

"We found him."

My phone pinged and I looked at the caller ID. Scarlett was calling me. I swiped talk.

"Scarlett?"

"He's in Italy!" she all but screamed.

"I think my guys were about to tell me the same thing. Are you heading out there?"

"Yes, on the first flight out."

"Do me a favor, will you?"

"Anything, Ransom. I'm so sorry I asked if you would stand by him."

"No worries. I need you to keep me informed when you get there. When he goes to his spot, the one by the restaurant, I want to know."

"You bet."

"And Scarlett?"

"Yes?"

"Don't tell him I'm coming."

I stared out the window of the jet and watched the sun's rays penetrate the clouds. It was an incredible sight. I had a feeling I'd be looking at the world in a new light. Not only for Sal, but for myself. I was going to have to deal with the bigots, and the ignorant people of this world. But honestly, wasn't that the case, anyway? Always some moron with no knowledge and a big mouth? I smiled to myself. It didn't matter. I would have Sal in my life.

The captain announced our descent and I wiped my hands on my jeans. I was nervous about seeing Sal again. I just hoped he didn't try to push me away again.

As soon as I landed, I grabbed a cab and went directly to the market place by my hotel. Something Buster had said to me during our time with Paul had stuck in my head and I was looking for something very specific to make my point. I finally found what I was looking for in one of the smaller shell shops and held my purchase with a grin. I checked into the hotel and alerted Scarlett to my presence in town. She texted me back immediately and let me know she'd keep her eyes and ears open. My phone pinged again and I looked at the caller ID.

Sebastian Lowery.

"Hello?"

"Ransom?"

"Well, you *did* call my number," I half-laughed since he sounded so surprised.

"Where are you?"

"Why?"

"I need you to come to Italy, Ransom. Sal is here and I —"

"I'm already here."

"Pardon?"

"I'm already here. I'm at the hotel Onda Verde."

"Why didn't you come straight to his parent's house?"

"Are we really going to discuss this now? I have my reasons. Now I told Scarlett the same thing I'm about to tell

167

you. He said he loves coming out to the Minerva. When he does, let me know."

"Hang on one second."

I tried to hear what was going on, but I suspected Sebastian had covered the phone with his hand. He was back on a few seconds later.

"Now is your chance. He just left."

"Thank you, Sebastian."

"No. Thank you, Ransom. You are the best thing that has happened to Sal in a very long time. You've made him smile — a real, genuine smile."

"I'll see you soon."

I took the short walk to the Minerva and headed down to the path below. I watched the boats bobbing up and down in the water and waited for the man of my dreams to find me.

I wasn't going to let him get away this time.

Chapter 15

SAL

I walked the path below the restaurant, watching the waves slowly break along the shore. The sunset was its usual glorious self, shooting rays of orange against the vast blue. Up ahead, a figure stood alone, hair waving gently in the wind. My stomach flipped, knotted, and my knees began to buckle. I could almost smell his cologne. I must have made a noise, because Ransom's shoulders straightened a bit. I strode over to him and stood by his side. He held a boat made of shells with little wine corks around the sides in his hand. I couldn't help but touch his shoulder.

"Ransom," I began.

"No." Ransom glanced over at me. "Follow me."

I walked beside him as we took the path around to the other side. Ransom motioned me to follow him down the stairs by the Africana Famous Club. We were at the very bottom of the stairs, the water slapping against the dock.

The wind gently caressed us; the smell of brine was strong. Ransom seemed to be in his own world staring out across the water and I was about to say something when he began to speak.

"Ships don't sink because of the water around them. Ships sink because of the water that gets *in* them." Ransom crouched down and placed the little boat in the water. It bobbed a bit against the waves, but found its bearings. "Don't let what's happening around you get inside you and weigh you down." Ransom stood and turned to face me. "You should have told me."

"I was scared. I didn't want to lose you, but at the same time, I couldn't keep you with me knowing what you'd face."

"I want to face it all, Sal, and I want to be by your side. You and you alone have the power to say this is not how your story is going to end. Fight, Sal, and I'll fight with you."

"You'll stay with me? Knowing how hard this is going to be?"

"If it doesn't challenge you, it won't change you. I want all the challenges that come with loving you, Sal. I want to wake up every morning raring to go, to start this new life with you. I'm looking forward to all the changes coming my way because, dammit, you're worth it."

I broke down and Ransom pulled me into his arms. I

held onto him. He was my life preserver in this rough storm, and I wouldn't let the water into our boat.

"I didn't think this would happen," I admitted. "I wanted you so much, but I knew I couldn't put you through all this."

"I'm here because I want to be. I've been to the doctor, followed his advice and I want to be with you, Sal. In every way possible."

"But —"

"No. No buts. Will we have to be careful? Of course, but I know what I'm in for and I'm not going anywhere. The second I saw you all those years ago, you stole my heart, Sal, and then I got to see you, the real you, and I was even more head over heels. You don't take credit for the things you do and I respect the hell out of you for it. You let an Irishman keep his pub, helped him pay his son's medical bills, and in the end, helped him put his son to rest. You showed up at a four-year-old's birthday party dressed as a squid. Those are the qualities which drew me to you, Sal. I knew you did a lot for the homeless, the LGBT and wounded vets, but all that additional information? It's just opened my eyes wider to the kind of man you are. You are the most extraordinary man I've ever met, Salvatore Falcon."

Ransom leaned in and brushed his lips against mine. I tried to move and he wrapped an arm around my waist, holding me firmly.

"No, you don't get to do that," he murmured against my lips. "Now kiss me, because I fucking missed you."

I wrapped my arms around him and finally kissed him back. Ransom groaned against my lips, biting at my lower lip before pulling me in closer and diving into my mouth. His taste, warmth, and scent enveloped my entire being. Ransom pulled out of the kiss slowly and I blinked, staring into his eyes.

"Is this real?" I whispered. "How did you know where I was?"

"It was a combination of Scarlett, Sebastian and my bodyguards. I wasn't going to let you run from me, Sal. Not when I just got you." Ransom held my face in his hands. "Where you go, I go. Got it? You don't get to decide what I do."

"Okay." I nodded. I couldn't believe he was here, that he'd flown all the way to Italy to find me. I knew what I felt for Ransom was more than lust. Truth was, I had fallen in love with him over the years. Then I got to meet him and the feeling was reinforced. Ransom searched my eyes and grinned, as if he knew what I was thinking.

"Yeah," he said huskily. "Me too."

I hugged him then. Nothing needed to be said.

We both knew.

We looked out over the water and I grinned at the

small boat holding its own against the waves. Even by itself, it conquered the rough seas.

I wasn't alone.

We walked back, hand in hand. I hadn't felt this way since the last time I'd seen him. He belonged with me — to me. I was about to start a new life and I was starting it with Ransom. By the time we got back to my parents', I could smell food cooking. I walked into the kitchen to find my parents, Scarlett and Sebastian smiling huge grins.

"I see you found your man." Sebastian nodded to me.

"Yes, I did."

"It is so good to meet you, Ransom." My mother took Ransom into her arms.

I glanced around the kitchen at my family and I knew things were going to be okay. They wouldn't be perfect, but I could live with that.

I would be living, and that was the bottom line.

I went with Ransom back to his hotel. We were going to stay there together for one night before we went back to my parents'. I sat on the queen-sized bed and couldn't tear my eyes away from Ransom. The shutters were open, bathing Ransom in an ethereal glow, and he'd never looked so beautiful to me. I shook as he undressed me. I was scared to death, but his touch soothed me, his eyes conveying so much in the moment. We kissed, touched, and breathed each other in. I wasn't ready for sex yet. I wanted to make sure we'd be safe when we finally did. Ransom cupped my cheek.

"Don't float away from me," he whispered. "I'm your anchor. I'll keep you safe during the storm."

I held him, inhaling the scent of his shampoo, the smell of the beach and a home-cooked meal.

"We're going to have a life, Sal. One filled with love."

"I want to come out," I blurted.

Ransom eased back, looking into my eyes. "I'm with you. Whatever you want to do, however you want to handle it. *I'm with you.*"

I kissed him then, tentatively, and he took charge. Our tongues tangled, breaths mixed and I'd never felt so right with anyone in my life.

Ransom's touch was light, seeking permission and waiting for me to give it. His hands swept up my thigh and across my chest. He was so warm, and I wrapped my arms around him, surrendering to his kiss. Being with Ransom was like nothing I've ever known.

Tomorrow was another day, and I'd be there to see it.

We headed back to my parents' the next morning. They were waiting for us. I helped Ransom bring his bags into the house and we went to the kitchen. Coffee was served and Sebastian looked deep in thought.

"What are you thinking, Sebastian?" I asked.

"I've been wanting to ask you this for a long time, and now that the situation is what it is, I'm going to throw it out there. How do you feel about TV?"

"You mean doing TV as opposed to movies?"

"Yes."

"I haven't thought much about it. Why?"

"I have an idea for a sitcom, a group of gay friends who hang out at a bar most of the time."

"So, a gay *Friends?*"

"Yes, partly. I've been talking to Scarlett about it and she's interested. When this idea came to me, I always had you in mind for the lead. You're the only one who can pull this off, Sal."

I glanced over at Ransom, who was grinning and nodding.

"Let me see what you have so far."

While we all sat around the table eating breakfast, I read Sebastian's script. I felt Ransom's presence in every way possible. Whether it was holding my hand, letting his hand rest on my thigh, or shoulder, he touched me as often as he could. I laughed out loud on more than one occasion and when I read the last page, I knew I'd be on board.

"I love it," I said.

"We could work on the pilot as soon as you'd like." Sebastian turned to Scarlett. "And you?"

"I've been a beard all these years, I can do it again in front of the camera."

Sebastian clapped his hands. "I love it!"

"One thing, though, Sebastian."

"Yes?"

I turned to look at Ransom. "It has to be filmed in Arizona."

"I can make it happen," Sebastian assured him with a wave of a hand.

"Are you sure?" Ransom whispered to me.

"Yes. I've never been surer."

"While you are here, why not take your friends on a tour, Salvatore?" my father spoke up.

"I think that would be great." Ransom kissed my cheek.

Chapter 16

The town of Praiano was breathtaking. I stood on the street, staring up at the houses built into the mountainside. Everything was mortar and rock and the streets were narrow with parking alongside the mountain. People passed by us on mopeds as we took the walk to the Minerva. I tried to take everything in at once, but it was impossible. We'd turn a corner and I would find something new to take my breath away. We were on a patio outside the bar and had a gorgeous view of the water.

"It's like time stands still here," I mused. "The water is so clear."

"Sal, you should take Ransom to Amalfi. Show him the sights," Sebastian suggested. "I'm going to take Scarlett out to the winery so you two can have some alone time."

"You don't have to do that. I'm happy with you guys being with us."

"No offense, gorgeous, but I'd like you and my bestie to spend some quality time together. We have plenty of time to spend together." Scarlett put an arm around Sal. "Isn't that right?"

"Yes." Sal took my hand. "We do."

"If you insist." I grinned, wrapping Sal up in my arms.

"All right. Come on, love, before you begin sobbing." Sebastian pulled her away.

I leaned on the railing with Sal at my side, watching the fishing boats bob up and down. Our fingers entwined and I sighed.

"You really need to see Amalfi at night. If you think this is beautiful, you have no idea."

"Oh, really?" I glanced over at him.

"Yes. Let's get a moped and drive alongside the coast. I guarantee you've never seen anything more beautiful."

"I'll have to take you to the edge of the world. Now that, my friend, is beauty."

"We'll have to see!"

Sal's face glowed with excitement. I loved seeing him like this, happy and carefree. I had no idea what he'd endured before we all rallied around him, but I wasn't going to let him fall back into his dark hole. Sal rented a moped and we were flying down the road, our laughter carrying on the wind. I let my head fall back and enjoyed the feel of Sal against my chest, my palms on his abdomen. The sunset was breathtaking, and as we came around another corner, my breath caught. Sal slowed down and stopped right above the town of Amalfi. Purple lights ran all along the docks and the lights from the nearby shops and hotels dotted the water.

"Oh, my God, Sal. It's unbelievable!"

"Come on!" Sal took my hand and we descended stairs to the docks below. We stood at the end and stared out across the water.

"I can see why you came here."

"It brings me peace in a way. It always has."

I turned to face him and took his hands. "You're not alone, Sal. Me, Sebastian, Scarlett, your parents — we're all here for you, okay? You don't ever have to do anything alone."

Sal nodded and I wiped the tear trickling down his cheek. I used to think crying was something only women did. I knew better now. It didn't make Sal any less of a man in my eyes. It made him more of a man.

"I'm doing it again," Sal sniffled.

"Hey, you want to cry, fucking cry, okay? I bawled when you dumped me, so don't ever think it's not okay to cry. I've always looked at it as releasing pain."

Sal blinked at me and then grinned. "I like that."

179

We sat at the end of the dock and talked for hours. Where we were going to go from there. I knew where I would be, with Sal. I didn't care if he moved to Arizona or stayed in California, I was going to make this work come hell or high water. I leaned against Sal's shoulder and watched the boats come in.

"We have to get back to reality soon." Sal sighed.

"Can I ask you something?"

"Sure."

"Do you know who gave you HIV?"

"I wish I did. The last time I was with someone, I was in disguise at a bar in San Francisco, one of the ones with back rooms where all sorts of stuff happens. I just wanted to get laid, scratch the itch. It was dark and I remember a guy coming up to me, grabbing my dick, and then spinning me into the wall face first. I know he was wearing a condom, because I heard him opening it and felt it. I'm going to have to play this very carefully. If I don't, people are going to come out of the woodwork saying I infected them."

"How many men have you been with?"

"Four, and I used protection with all of them. I swear."

"I believe you. I've used protection with every woman I've been with."

"Do I want to know how many?"

"I'm not going to lie to you. It's a hell of a lot, Sal." I moved back a bit to look him in the eye. "Do you still want me?"

"What kind of question is that? Of course I do. Who you slept with before me is just that: before me. I want us to be exclusive, though. No more fucking around."

"I wouldn't want to be with anyone else, Sal. That's the God's-honest truth." I looked out over the water with a grin. "Tell me something no one else knows about you."

"Once, I snuck out of one movie theater and into another without paying."

I laughed and kissed him lightly. "Is that the worst thing you've ever done?"

"No, once I hid my mother's birth control pills because I wanted a sibling." Sal laughed lightly. "How is it having a younger brother? Did you drive each other crazy?"

I told Sal all about how Gareth was born prematurely, how I didn't know if he'd be there every day I went to visit, how I cried at night and prayed to God not to take my little brother.

"He told me to go all out for you," I admitted with a grin. "He told me I had to let him go live his life. He's right, you know. I've always felt responsible for him, especially after my mother died and my father started using drugs. I was more than just his older brother and I guess I've been kinda living life but not really living it. When I saw you that first night, I knew my feelings were never going to go away. Even though I'd never met you, when I was a kid, I used to sit in my room at night and dream of ways I could actually meet you. How I would make you see the real me, and you'd fall in love with me and we'd live happily ever after. You'd take me and Gareth out of our life and make it a better one."

Sal leaned over and kissed me softly. I closed my eyes and just let the sensation of his warm lips wash over me. I loved how he kissed me — touched me.

"If I had known you back then, I think I would have fallen for you," Sal murmured against my lips.

"When we hit it big, I think my first thought was somehow, someway, I could finally meet you — and then I did. That night at Sebastian's, I was scared out of my mind."

Sal cupped my cheek and looked into my eyes. "You were the most gorgeous person in the room. I didn't see anyone but you."

We kissed then for what seemed like hours. I couldn't get enough of Sal. We finally left Amalfi and headed back to Sal's parents' house. They had dinner on the table and were sitting around it, laughing, and drinking wine.

"How did your tour go?" Sebastian winked.

"It was perfect," I answered.

After dinner, Sal and I sat on the patio holding hands. The moon was high in the sky and it was so peaceful. Not a sound carried on the wind.

"Tell me about your mom," Sal said, breaking the silence.

"She was beautiful, a mixture of Gareth and me. She had the softest hair. I don't know what she used, but she always smelled like lavender when she came out of the bathroom. Whenever Gareth and I were sick, she'd lay in bed with us and run her fingers through our hair. Every Sunday, she'd pull out this yellow dress with flowers on it and we would sit in the back yard and talk about what we were thankful for. That was her way of avoiding church, I think. When she got sick, she would always have a smile for us. We would sit in bed with her and show her our homework, read books and play board games. I think the worst part for her was when she lost her hair. I remember her crying with a chunk of it in her hand and I took it and put a rubber band around the end of it. I still have it in a box of things I just couldn't get rid of. It still smells like lavender."

"You miss her." Sal laced his fingers with mine.

"I do, but there are times I know she's with me. There'll be this light gust of wind and I swear I can smell lavender."

"She is with you, and she sees the wonderful man you've become. I know she's proud of you, because I am."

"You are?"

"Look at you, who you've become, how you are. Of course she's proud."

"Will you… go with me to meet my father?"

"Of course."

I searched his eyes, and touched his face lightly. There was so much to read in Salvatore Falcon's eyes, it almost scared me. This man was everything to me.

"When we get back," I said.

"When we get back." Sal nodded.

I woke up alone and rolled over in the bed. Sal and I had kissed most of the night, holding each other, and lightly touching. As soon as we got back to the States though, I was going to show him how I felt. I wasn't scared about being with him, I knew he was mine and I was right where I belonged. I headed out to the kitchen to find Sal's mother puttering over the stove. She smiled as I came in and motioned to the coffeepot.

"Salvatore said you like your coffee strong."

"Yes, thank you, Mrs. Falcon."

"Ah ah!" She wagged a finger at me. "You call me Aria." She smiled, placing a plate on the counter. I peered over to see an egg right in the middle of a piece of bread. "Looks good. Where is Sal?"

"He and Sebastian left early this morning for a run. He said you needed your rest." She took a cup of coffee for herself and another plate and sat down. I joined her and she grinned at me over her coffee cup.

"You are in love with my boy."

I nodded.

"Good. He needs someone to love him. He has been alone much of his life, never knowing if someone wished to be with him for money or fame. Even if you were not famous or had money, I would know that you are in love with my Salvatore. The way you look at him says it all. He has told me a bit about your family, how you lost your mother. I am so sorry for your loss."

"Thank you. It has been a long time now, but sometimes it feels fresh."

"A mother's love is not replaceable, Ransom. As a mother, I know I would give my life to save my son's." She took my hand. "I would never try to replace your mother's love, but I *can* love you as my own."

"Thank you," I whispered.

"You are good for my boy." She patted my hand with

185

a smile. "Maybe you can talk him into having children."

"W-What?" I almost spit out my coffee.

"I did not say today, Ransom." She grinned. "Have you ever thought about children?"

I couldn't say I hadn't. I always wondered what it would be like to have a little me running around. How I would do things differently.

"I have," I admitted.

"Well, you must marry Salvatore first," she laughed.

"Of course!"

"If you do, you must have it here."

"I wouldn't marry him anywhere else, I promise."

"Good. Now eat up."

Chapter 17

SAL

Getting back to the States was a bit nerve wracking. Sebastian had gone back to L.A. to start making his show a reality and I went back to Flagstaff with Ransom. He'd been patient with me as far as sex was concerned, but the thing I wanted most of all was to be closer to him. My fear was the only thing keeping me from making a move on him. It was mid-January and snow blanketed Flagstaff. Living in California, I hadn't seen it except when I went up into the mountains. Ransom pulled up to a house and I got out, taking a look around. Pine trees heavy with the weight of snow surrounded his property. Pinecones dotted the ground and I stepped into a bed of pine needles. The air was crisp and clean and I inhaled sharply.

"The altitude is going to fuck with you for a while," Ransom said, as he came around the car and took my hand.

"It's beautiful, Ransom. The air is so clean."

"Come on inside."

I followed Ransom into the house and stood in the foyer. For someone who had a lot of money, you wouldn't have guessed it from Ransom's house. The living room was spacious, but not overcrowded. It held a sectional couch positioned right in front of a large fireplace. Pictures dotted the log walls and a TV sat above an alcove full of books and CDs.

"Wow! This is awesome. It's all log?"

"Yep. Gareth has a treehouse and I have a log home. Come see the kitchen."

I walked behind Ransom, admiring the view of his luscious ass. He glanced over his shoulder with a knowing look and I blushed at being caught ogling him. He headed for the coffeemaker and I relaxed against his kitchen island. The whole kitchen had a homey feeling. The cabinets were made of pine as well as the island counter. A rack of pots hung from the ceiling above the island and four knotty pine chairs circled it. I sat down and looked around.

"I figured we'd sit in front of the fireplace and tell stories." Ransom winked at me.

"Oh? Like what?"

"I really want to hear all about making movies and stuff."

"I'll tell you whatever you want to know."

Ransom made two cups of coffee and we settled in

front of the fireplace. Ransom lit the fire and we reclined against the couch. Our fingers entwined and I looked down at our joined hands.

"I never thought I'd be here," I admitted.

"I never thought you'd be here." Ransom tilted his head at me as it rested against the couch cushions.

"We have so much to learn about each other."

"Well, I know your mom wants kids." Ransom chuckled.

"Oh hell." I sighed and then laughed. "She brought up the grandkids to you?"

"I told her I'd marry you first." Ransom grew serious.

"You'd... *marry me*?"

"Yes, but I'm keeping my last name." Ransom grinned, leaning over to kiss me. "You don't want to get married?"

"I only saw myself marrying you. Of course, that was in my dreams."

"Well, I'm going to make it a reality — when you're ready, of course."

I turned to view him face to face. "You're serious?"

"I couldn't be more serious right now. I know we have a long way to go, but I know who you are, Salvatore Falcon."

"My answer will be yes." I squeezed his fingers.

"Good. We'll be married in Italy."

"Of course."

Ransom laughed and eyed me. "So? What can you tell me that most people don't know about movie making?"

"It's a lot of standing around, actually. They film one scene, and then move all the cameras around to get every angle. Also, the music you hear in bar scenes and stuff? There really isn't any music, they put it in later."

"Really? So you're pretending to dance?"

"Yup. That's why in some movies you're laughing your ass off at people who look like they have no rhythm."

"That explains a lot."

"Don't get me started on sex scenes." I blew out a breath. "I mean, try being intimate with a whole bunch of people in the room and a camera right in your face. It's so damn technical there's no room for attraction." I laughed.

"So, this new show. Do you think you'll have love scenes?"

"If I do, you can rest assured no one will replace you in my life, Ransom. You are it for me."

"As long as I know I'm your one and only, I can handle anything."

I leaned in and Ransom met me halfway. We kissed softly, our lips moving over each other's, tongues teasing. I gently eased Ransom on his back and hovered above him. He was hard and so was I, but I wasn't ready, not just yet. Ransom smiled and touched my face in understanding.

"I know," he whispered. "Don't worry. I'll wait, Sal."

I settled beside him, watching the flames flicker in the fireplace. It was comfortable, with the snow falling outside and the fire inside. It felt like home more than my own house ever did.

"I want you here with me, Sal."

"I'm here, Ransom," I assured him.

I had a lot to do, and I needed to get a few things done very quickly, like telling the world I was gay and had HIV. I'd seen what it had done to a few celebrities — blackmail and payouts. I wasn't going to let that happen. People were going to find out on my terms and in my own way. I nestled into Ransom and closed my eyes, listening to his heartbeat.

"How about I show you around tomorrow?" Ransom murmured into my hair.

"I'd love it."

After drinking our coffee, Ransom showed me the rest of his house. I loved it immediately. He had one room for his music, where guitars and a drum set lined one wall. The room next to it held some gym equipment and an aged chest of drawers.

"That was my mom's. The one thing I kept from our old house," he explained. "Most of the stuff is in storage, but this is where she kept all her special belongings."

"Have you looked through it?"

"Just the top drawer. I haven't had the balls to look any further."

"Maybe we'll do it together someday." I took his hand.

"Sure. Come on, let me show you the rest of the house."

We finally got to his bedroom and I smiled at the king-sized bed against one wall. A TV was on the opposite wall, held up by what appeared to be stained and varnished pallets.

"Are those..." I motioned to them.

"Yep. Pallets. We have a friend in town who can make anything out of a pallet. Rebel's living room is just one large pallet against one wall. It has space for a TV, books, and CDs. He loves that thing." Ransom walked into the bathroom and began undressing. I stood there, awed. Ransom was lean but defined. He wasn't sporting six-pack abs and huge biceps, but he was built nicely. He had the most gorgeous dick I'd ever seen. It hung low, smacking his thigh as he moved around. A light dusting of hair covered his nuts and I think I started drooling. Ransom took my hand and began undressing me. We got in the shower and I leaned against his back, enjoying the feel of skin against mine. He wrapped his arms around me and I sighed in contentment.

"Our life is just beginning, Sal," Ransom whispered

into my ear. "I can't wait to show you everything."

I held his hands against my abdomen as he began kissing up the side of my neck. His hand drifted to my rapidly rising prick and began to stroke me. I wanted to be with him more than anything, wanted to feel his dick fill me inside. I'd always been a bottom, and I wanted Ransom in my ass. I came quickly, spurting all over myself and Ransom's hand. He moved us under the spray and kissed me as we rinsed off.

"Are you a bottom, Sal?" Ransom asked, as he dried me off.

"Yes."

"Well, in that case, I can't wait to take your ass." He winked.

"You have no idea."

We lie in bed, just staring at each other in the light of the moon. Ransom's ceiling was basically a skylight. You could see every constellation in the sky right from his bed.

"Will you go with me to see Paul tomorrow?"

"Of course. He doesn't hate me, does he?"

"No. He wants me to be happy. I called him from the plane to let him know we'd worked things out."

I closed my eyes as Ransom pulled me into his chest. This was right. I felt it from the tip of my toes to my hair. It was natural to be with Ransom, out in the open, and fuck what anyone else said.

"Sleep well, Sal Falco," Ransom whispered.

I would now.

Morning came, and I was in Ransom's car on our way to the hospital. We stopped at some coffee place Ransom swore was better than Starbucks and I ordered one of their specials. By the time we got to the hospital, I was bouncing all over the place. Ransom just laughed and took my hand as we entered the hospital. The nurse at the desk laughingly told us Paul was in the courtyard with the other residents having a snowball fight. Ransom spoke with the doctor and I excused myself. I walked out and barely missed a snowball meant for my head. I twirled around to see one of the residents with a hand over her mouth.

"Oops! I'm so sorry!" she squeaked.

"No problem," I laughed, wiping the snow from my jacket.

"She has terrible aim."

I turned back to find Paul leaning against one of the pillars, grinning.

"Hey, Paul." I extended my hand and he pulled me into a hug.

"How ya doin', Sal?"

"I'm great. Better than great, actually."

"Walk with me."

Paul began to walk across the courtyard and I followed. He stopped in front of a large tree and looked up.

"This tree has been right here for over a hundred years. They wanted to chop it down when they built this place, but in the end, they decided it would stand for something. After all this time, it still grows — still stands tall. It takes a beating from the elements and yet it still manages to survive — to thrive even. We are like this tree, Sal. We take a beating and we come back fighting. You have one hell of a guy at your side and I think he's finally able and ready to give his whole heart to you, so don't fuck it up."

"You love him," I said.

Paul glanced over at me. "I think part of me will always love him, but not the way you love him or he loves you. Now, it's more of a brotherly kind of love. I know his heart is taken. Hell — I knew it the first time he ever laid eyes on you. Ransom is the kind of man who loves with every part of his being. Be worthy of that love, Sal."

"We haven't said that yet."

"You don't have to. He's willing to do anything for you. I saw it when he came to see me after you broke his heart. He had that look in his eyes, like it wasn't over, he

195

was going to do whatever it took to have you in his life. That man is tenacious as hell. It's how he was able to raise Gareth on his own, how he got the band where we are, how he keeps us all together now. We're a family, Sal. Now you're part of it too."

"I'm honored, you know."

"Good. I like you, Sal, and I think you're good for him and he for you. Whatever comes your way, you'll face it together and be stronger for it." Paul glanced over his shoulder with a grin. "Excuse me for just a sec."

I leaned against the tree as Paul grabbed some snow and made a ball out of it.

"Be right back," he laughed as he began running.

I crossed my arms with a grin, watching Paul chase after the other residents. Ransom walked out and a snowball smacked against his head. He roared in laughter and prepared his own.

"He's right, you know."

"Jesus!" I grabbed my chest as a voice came from behind me. I looked around the tree to find Buster behind the fence. "What the fuck!"

"Just keeping you on your toes, Sal. It's good to see you and Ransom together."

"You need a hobby," I said in exasperation.

"This is my hobby. Watching out for Paul."

I narrowed my eyes and fixed him with a look. "If I

didn't know any better, I'd say you had feelings for Paul."

"I'm not allowed to have feelings, Sal. Besides — I don't think I know how to feel anymore."

I walked over to the fence and held the bars, searching his face. "What happened to you?"

"Stuff that happens in nightmares. I came out of the fight with a shade of darkness surrounding me. It will always be there."

"You're a good guy, Buster."

"It's Kirk."

"I think I like Buster better. Are you everywhere?" I joked.

"I'm where I'm needed, Sal. Right now, that's with Paul. He's got a long road ahead of him. You don't just get rid of PTSD. It will haunt you."

"Why do I think you know a lot about the subject?" Buster didn't answer, but his gaze flicked to Paul behind me. I didn't have to turn to look. I just knew. A small smile played at his lips and I turned around to see Paul smashing snow into Ransom's face. When I turned back, Buster was gone. Ransom came up behind me and wrapped his arms around me.

"Come play in the snow."

"I'm not really equipped for it."

"We'll have to stop in town and get you some gear, but for now, you can use my gloves."

Ransom handed me his gloves and I marveled at his face. His cheeks were red from the cold and his eyes were bright with mirth.

"Go easy on me. I didn't get to play in the snow a lot."

"You'll learn fast," Ransom laughed, taking my hands and pulling me along. "Just duck and cover."

I laughed as I joined the fight. For just a few hours, I could forget about all the bad in my life and look at all the good. I had to stop thinking about what I didn't have and see what I did.

Chapter 18

SAL

Ransom took me all over Flagstaff after we left the hospital. I knew he'd made an appointment for both of us to be seen by his doctor in town. It was sweet of him to want to learn all he could about HIV and how to be with me safely. I needed to call my own doctor and have my care transferred to Flagstaff. It was still early enough in the day and the sun was still high in the sky. Ransom kept driving and I noticed there weren't as many houses the further we went and then I saw the sign for the North Rim of the Grand Canyon. I glanced over at him to see him with a smile.

"I've never been to the Grand Canyon," I admitted.

"Well, you will now. It's usually closed for the winter, but I called in a favor."

"Oh, did you now?"

"Yup."

I couldn't believe the change. Trees sprung up

everywhere and the scenery was gorgeous. Ransom drove for what seemed like hours until we came to a small shop on the side of the road. He parked and we got out. Tables featured Native American art and jewelry and Ransom peered down at one of the pieces.

"I'd like this one please." He pointed.

I looked down to see a Phoenix bird, wings spread, carved from some kind of stone.

"It's beautiful."

"It's yours." Ransom handed over the money and placed the stone in my hand. "You hang on to that for strength."

We continued on and once again, Ransom pulled into a stop on the side of the road. We walked along a path and then Ransom pulled me close as we got right up to the barrier. I looked out into a canyon of beauty.

"Jinx loves it here. His grandpa used to bring him up here all the time. He's the only guy I know who pays to pick up exactly one rock."

"He pays?" I asked.

"Yes. You're not allowed to take rocks, but he contributes a shit ton of money every year so they allow him one once a year. He came here with Jayden not too long ago, so he's done for the year."

"It's pretty important to him, I take it."

"It's kind of like an homage to his grandpa, but I can

200

see why he comes every year. It's breathtaking isn't it?"

Red peeked out from behind white and I could still see some of the green alongside the canyon. It truly was a spectacle. I inhaled deeply, taking in everything around me.

"Life renews itself. I've seen it happen repeatedly. I've seen a fire rage through and life comes back even stronger. I always said after my mother died I would live every day as if it were my last, but somewhere along the way, I forgot. I have you now, Sal, and I plan to live every day to its damn fullest." Ransom extended his hand and placed it on mine. "We're going to rock the shit out of this."

I laughed and Ransom turned me to face him, cupped my face, and kissed me. I reveled in his warmth and taste. Life couldn't get any better than this. I was standing in front of beauty, both the canyon and Ransom.

We drove back into town and Ransom took a side street, parking in front of a bar.

"What's this?" I asked.

"The Green Room. You'll love it. We play here now and then when we come back into town. The guys who own it are old friends."

We entered the bar and I took a look around. The bar itself was to the right and ran the length of the entire place. High-backed wooden stools pushed up against the bar and a pool table and seating area faced it.

"Yo, Tyler! A Recycling Bin please!" Ransom

shouted.

"And a Recycling Bin is?"

"It's a drink, but normally I only have one or I'll be up all night. It's got a can of Red Bull stuck in it upside down."

"Okayyy." I laughed.

"You can have a sip."

We sat at the bar and shot the shit with the guy Ransom had referred to as Tyler. Another man joined us and they both stared at me.

"Hey, guys?" Ransom waved his hand in front of their faces. "I'm a pretty big deal here, too, ya know?"

"Yeah, but that's Sal Falco," Brandon said slowly. "In our bar."

"I plan on spending a lot of time here, guys. You're going to see me quite a bit."

"He's with me, guys." Ransom lifted his brows.

"Like, *with* with?" Brandon's mouth dropped open.

"Yes. *With*," I clarified.

"Holy shit," Tyler whispered.

"I know, right?" Ransom chuckled.

"Dude. I would have never pegged you as gay," Brandon said to me.

"That was the idea."

"And you pegged me?" Ransom shot them an amused grin.

"Nah. Didn't have any clue, Ransom." Tyler shook his head.

"Well, you're welcome any time, Mr. Falco. Drinks on the house whenever you want."

"Just call me Sal." I grinned.

"You got it." Tyler smiled.

"Look guys, a lot of stuff is about to come out, so we need to keep this on the down low, okay?" Ransom leaned over the bar and looked Brandon and Tyler in the eyes. "I mean *really* low."

"You bet, Ransom. You know we don't put up with gossip or reporters."

"Look, I really want to tell you guys the truth before you see it on the news —" I began.

"Sal." Ransom shook his head.

"They have the right to know." I motioned them closer and told them about everything. Brandon sympathized with me, as his brother had had HIV for six years after being infected by an ex-girlfriend. Tyler was the same. Neither one of them judged me and it felt so damned freeing. They didn't look at me differently even after they'd heard my secret. For the first time in weeks, I could breathe normally. I had a feeling I'd come to the right place with the right man.

"Hey, you and the guys going to play tonight?" Brandon asked.

"Will you?" I asked hopefully.

"Sure. Let me get the guys over here."

Ransom was on his phone and I noticed Tyler staring at me. I lifted a brow and grinned.

"Yes?"

"I can't believe you're sitting in my bar," he said sheepishly as he shook his head.

"*Our* bar," Brandon interrupted.

"So, they play here a lot?" I asked.

"Oh, yeah."

A half-hour later, the guys walked in and the crowd went crazy whistling, and clapping. Harley, Jinx, Gareth, and Rebel surrounded me within seconds. They patted me on the back and hugged me, welcoming me into their family. They all discussed what song they wanted to play and Harley grinned.

"You know what I want to play."

"And we always do what you want?" Rebel arched both brows.

"Yep." Harley nodded. "It's a rule."

"All right, we do Harley's fave!" Ransom yelled.

"And that would be?" I asked.

"Fall Out Boy, *Sugar, We're Goin' Down.*"

"I like that song!" I admitted.

"Well, then hang on." Ransom winked.

The guys left for the stage and their significant others

joined me. Well, Rebel didn't have a significant other. Ransom had said Rebel wasn't the relationship type. I sat on one of the stools and watched as Ransom got up on stage. I had Jinx's main squeeze on one side and Gareth's husband on the other.

"Isn't he just...wow." Jayden sighed.

"Who? Ransom?" I elbowed him playfully.

"He *is* pretty hot. Not as hot as my Jinx, though." Jayden winked.

My attention was on the stage as the guys began to play. Harley and Ransom sang in perfect harmony. It was impressive how close the guys were and how well they worked together. I knew the story: they'd known each other since grade school and had grown up together, playing in each other's garages. Ransom had a presence that couldn't be denied — which is why he was the lead singer. But I'd heard an interview once where they admitted all of them could sing. The crowd was singing along and Jayden dragged me up front. Ransom looked like a god up on stage. The guys played a few more songs off their own album and I felt like a kid again.

We left close to one in the morning and I was exhausted. By the time Ransom pulled up to his house, I was half-asleep. We had to be at the doctor's in the morning and I needed about ten hours of sleep. I threw off my clothes in the bedroom and crawled under the covers.

Ransom slid into the other side of the bed and immediately pulled me into his arms.

"Did you have fun?" he asked.

"I did. Thank you so much for today, Ransom. I feel like I've been on the go for a week, though." I yawned.

"You'll get used to the altitude, and then you won't feel so tired."

"Ransom?"

"Yeah?"

"Thank you. I mean it. I felt so... normal today."

"You're far from it, Sal, but I know what you mean. Get some rest. We have another full day tomorrow."

" 'K." I nodded.

Then, I was out like a light.

I was on the phone with Sebastian in the morning. Ransom was making breakfast in his sweatpants. He was sexy no matter what he wore. I shot him a salacious look. He shook his butt at me and got back to what he was doing on the stove.

"Sal, are you listening to me?"

"Yeah, I'm here."

"I've got everything set up for you. You'll be doing a press conference in front of one of the LGBT youth homes, just as you asked."

"Good. People need to be made aware that our gay youth are suffering."

"I think once this all comes out, you'll have a huge weight off your shoulders, Sal. This is good; don't think it's not. It's going to show you who your real friends are."

"Thank you, Sebastian, for everything."

"Of course."

I hung up and enjoyed watching Ransom. He moved effortlessly, the soft fabric stretching across his mouth-watering globes.

"Stop staring at my ass." Ransom glanced over his shoulder.

"Can't help it. I want to lick it."

"Maybe later." Ransom wiggled his brows at me.

"So, are you going with me?"

Ransom turned around and gave me his full attention. "Of course I am."

"You'll be outing yourself."

"And?"

"I just didn't want to presume."

"Look." Ransom came over and pulled me into his arms. "I am yours. You are mine. Where you go, I go. What hurts you, hurts me. I'm in this for however long we're on the Earth together."

"Okay." I nodded.

"Now, we have a doctor's appointment, so get your butt in the shower."

"Oh yeah. I was so tired I didn't even shower last night."

"I did this morning, so go on now. By the time you're done, I should have all of this ready for you."

I got up and strode across the kitchen. I stopped and turned around. "Ransom?"

"Yes?"

"You are one hell of a man."

"So are you." Ransom smiled.

I walked to the bathroom and stared in the mirror. My life was about to change even more. The difference was this time, I was ready for it.

After the doctor, we ended up at Harley's house, where it seemed we were all meeting for dinner. I stood in the backyard, smiling at the guitar-shaped pool. I'd heard all about Harley from Ransom and my heart ached for his own personal trials. Now he had Achilles at his side, though, and Achilles' parents loved Harley to death. I sensed a presence next to me and glanced over to see the band manager, Stan, staring out at the night sky.

"Hey," I said.

"You're a good man, Sal." He looked over at me. "Sebastian called me, wanted to know if I could look into real estate for him. You're seriously going to film a sitcom out here?"

"Yes. It keeps me close to Ransom and I want out of L.A." I searched his eyes. "What is it?"

"I have a great deal of respect for you. You're doing exactly what you want. The guys will have your back when you come out."

"I feel like such a hypocrite." I sighed.

"I don't know how Hollywood is, but I've heard it's forgiving — for the right star. I would worry more about your fans than the press, though."

"I am." I nodded. "I'm going to make it up to them."

"Well, I've heard nothing but the best from Ransom and the guys about you."

I stared at him closely. God, he reminded me of someone and I couldn't put my finger on it.

"What?" Stan grinned. "Do I have something on my face?"

"No, you just look like someone I know, but I can't pinpoint who."

"Ah, I guess I have one of those faces."

Whistling came from the house and I looked over my shoulder to see Ransom waving at me.

"Seems dinner is ready."

"Let's get to it."

Chapter 19

SAL

I was nervous as I stood in front of the LGBT youth center in downtown Los Angeles. I knew what I was doing was for the best, but a part of me was scared to death. Reporters were everywhere and the street was blocked off for my very special announcement. Ransom squeezed my hand as I cleared my throat and looked out over all the expectant faces. My eyes fell on the band members in the front, along with Jinx's boyfriend's band, Sebastian, and Fergus and Maggie from the Irish diner. Fergus winked at me and I smiled at them. I'd tried to call my manager before I came back to L.A. but he never answered. I left him a voicemail saying he was fired. Dr. Holt was also in attendance; he was there to answer any HIV questions should they arise. I took a deep breath and began.

"I owe you all an apology. For years I've been playing a role, one I shouldn't have, one of a straight man."

There were gasps within the crowd and I continued.

"That all changes today. I refuse to hide anymore. If I never make another movie, I'm okay with it. A few weeks ago, I found out I have HIV. I felt it would be best if I cleared the air about everything. You all deserve that. I wanted to address this before it became public knowledge and twisted beyond belief. I am healthy, I am in love, and more than anything, I have a new outlook on life. When I got my diagnosis, I ran. I left people who were there for me and now I know I'm going to need them more than ever. I am retiring from making films for a bit, but I do have something in the works with Sebastian Lowery, so I ask you to be patient. We'll bring you something that's needed."

I glanced over at Ransom to see him give me a brief nod.

"Now, I will take your questions."

I answered questions for two hours and I made sure I took them from the public first. The reporters had to wait, and that was another thing Ransom and I had agreed on. The public needed attention before anyone else. They bought tickets to my movies. They made me who I am today. I owed them a huge debt. Ransom and I answered questions together about our relationship and I was surprised at how the crowd reacted to my news. They weren't upset in the least bit. I knew it wouldn't always be this way. I knew there would always be some small-minded individuals, but I also knew I could deal with it. I waved to the crowd as I left the podium with Ransom. We walked into the youth center and applause came from everywhere. Ransom grinned at me and I wiped my eyes.

"Thank you all so much," I choked out.

"We stand with you, Mr. Falco!" one of the kids shouted.

"Thank you so much. Now, let's get down to making some food!"

More applause came and Ransom leaned into my ear. "This is about my comment about doing more?"

"No. This is about me taking responsibility. You weren't wrong. Writing a check is easy. Getting into the thick of it takes work, and I plan on working."

"And that right there is why I love you."

My head whipped around to Ransom and my mouth dropped open. That was the first time he'd said the words.

"Don't look so surprised." Ransom cupped my cheek. "You had to know."

"Kiss him!" one of the kids shouted.

I laughed and grabbed Ransom's face in my hands. "I love you too."

And then I kissed him.

In front of everyone.

And it felt so damned good.

We spent hours at the youth center, mostly just hanging out with the kids and talking about their lives. I felt I had a duty to them now. They needed to know they weren't forgotten; that people such as Ransom and I would be there for them throughout everything. Both of us wrote a huge check to the youth center for bedding, food, and toiletries. I wanted to do whatever I could. We left through the back door, with one of Ransom's bodyguards holding open the limo door.

"Hammer." Ransom nodded to the large man as he entered the limo.

"Hammer?" I repeated.

"You don't want to know." Ransom slid into the seat. I heard a soft chuckle from the bodyguard before the door closed, sealing us in. We pulled onto the street and noticed some of the news vans still alongside the curb.

"So, I'm putting both houses up for sale. Scarlett is moving to Arizona as well."

"She is? When did she agree to that?"

"When I told her I was leaving. She didn't want the house and she's sick of L.A."

"So, you'll be moving in with me?" Ransom asked.

I could hear the hope in his voice and I grinned, running the pad of my thumb across his bottom lip.

"I wouldn't live anywhere else."

We ended up at my house on the beach. I was going to have all my belongings packed and auction off some stuff for the LGBT youth center.

I stood in the bedroom, staring out at the beach. My life had gone from lonely, to scared, to feeling loved. Arms wrapped around me from behind and I leaned back into Ransom's warmth.

"It's a beautiful view."

"I always loved the fact I could look out, but no one could see in."

"Well, I'm glad they can't see in, because I'm about to make love to you."

"Ransom, I —"

"No, Sal. It's time. I want to show you just how much you mean to me. We've both seen the doctor, and we both know how to proceed, so please stop pushing me away."

"I'm scared."

Ransom cupped my face in his hands. "You don't need to be."

I was shaking like a leaf as Ransom touched me. My

shirt fell to the floor and then Ransom began unzipping my pants. I stilled his hand, took a deep breath, and searched his eyes.

"Hey," he said softly. "It's okay. We're going to be safe. I want to be with you."

I nodded slowly, swallowing the huge lump in my throat. I had avoided sex as long as I could, but in the end, Ransom wasn't going to buy any of my excuses. I closed my eyes as his warm lips traveled up the racing pulse in my throat. His hand slid down my spine and to my ass cheek. He squeezed it, pulling me closer to him. His skin was soft and I buried my face in his neck as he wrapped me up in his warmth. I'd never felt the way I did now with anyone but Ransom. I felt safe, warm, and loved. My jeans fell to the floor along with my boxers and Ransom trailed a path down my abdomen, leaving light kisses as he removed the denim from around my ankles.

I tried to breathe normally, but I found myself gasping at his touches on my super-sensitive body. Ransom maneuvered me to the bed and I sat down; his weight came down on top of me and pushed me back. He hovered there for a few seconds, a small smile playing on his lips. He trailed his fingers alongside my ribcage and goose bumps blew out all over me. His lips lowered to mine and I opened up, allowing him in. I was so lost in the kiss, I didn't realize he'd slipped two fingers inside me. I rode them, gasping at the sensations in my body. Ransom kept his mouth firmly attached to mine as he worked me, brought me to the brink, and then removed his fingers. I was breathing hard and seeing spots as I watched him sheath his dick and squirt some lube on his length, adding some to my hole. The realization of what we were about to do hit me and I began to panic.

"Wait!" I blurted.

"No." Ransom positioned himself at my hole and edged inside. "You're not going to overthink this, you're not going to worry about anything. The only thing I want from you is to finally have the pleasure you've been denying yourself."

And then he was inside me and my heart beat out of my chest. My eyes rolled back at every stroke, the punch to my prostate had me crying out. I held on to him as if he was my life preserver. We rocked together, passionate kisses and stolen breaths. Ransom held my face as he rocked into me, my mouth opened in a silent scream, and he covered it, taking my mouth with force. I wrapped my legs around his hips, locking my ankles together. I'd never felt anything like it. His girth stretched me deliciously and his length knocked my sweet spot every single time. I was so overwhelmed, I couldn't breathe. Ransom slowed down his rhythm, gently touching my cheek and kissing me softly.

"I want to do this every night," he murmured against

my lips. "I want you to know I'm not scared, Sal, and you shouldn't be either."

Ransom pulled out, and then snapped his hips forward and I lost control of everything. I came crying out, my legs shaking against him, and Ransom sunk his full length into me three more times before crying out himself. We stayed there, gasping for air and sweating. Ransom smoothed away my hair from my forehead and smiled at me.

"Now *that* was awesome!"

"Holy hell," I panted.

"Yeah? I lost my man virgin card with you." He waggled his brows.

"I lost my never-been-in-love-card with *you*." I grinned.

"I think this was fate, Sal. I'll be here, through it all, good times and bad."

I held him then. I didn't know how to thank him for everything he'd given up for me. He was going to be ridiculed, and I was the cause of it.

"Stop it," Ransom whispered. "I swear I can hear you overthinking again."

"How do you know me so well?"

"I've watched you from the age of twelve. I love your laugh, your scent, and your touch. When we finally met, I swear I heard a click, like our hearts finally joined."

I grinned and Ransom's cheeks reddened. "I sounded so girlie just then, didn't I?"

"Nah. Who said men always have to be macho? Is there a rule somewhere that says we can't cry or say romantic things? My father is very romantic with my mother and he cried the day I was born. Does that make him less of a man? I don't think so."

"You're right, but just in case, I'm going to get up and do some sit-ups."

I laughed as Ransom pulled out carefully and removed the condom. He walked to the bathroom and I heard the toilet flush. Then he was back, with a warm washcloth. He cleaned me off and then jumped back on the bed, pulling me close to him. I think he was laughing.

"What is it?" I asked.

"I'm excited. I can't wait for us to start this incredible journey together."

"The heavy metal rocker and the actor," I mused.

"You should make a movie."

"Maybe someday I will. A huge gay movie!"

"As long as I get to play the rocker."

"I'll make sure you get acting lessons right away." I touched his face, smiling at the mirth in his eyes.

"Who says I can't act?" Ransom lifted both brows.

"We'll start small. Maybe a guest appearance on the sitcom."

"I like that idea."

"I have a good feeling about it. The script is hilarious."

"It's going to be a hit, just wait." Ransom rolled on top of me and kissed my nose. "Anything you do is fabulous."

"I think I'm going to pick Grandpa's brain for one-liners. According to Rebel, that man has some whoppers."

"Oh, God, don't get me started."

I laughed.

Chapter 20

Sal was fitting quite nicely into my life. It was so easy being with him, laughing with him — loving with him. The guys loved him and he came with me to practice sessions on more than one occasion. I loved watching him rock it out, banging his head to the music. He was so alive, his face flush with sweat. He was the most gorgeous man I'd ever seen.

And he was mine.

The bodyguards were now watching out for Sal, too, but in Flagstaff no one gave a shit. Sal was just Sal and everyone treated him like one of the guys. Sebastian was working his ass off trying to get his studio up and running and most of the town folks who knew anything about construction had come to help. A house was bought to shoot the scenes when the characters were at home and right next door was the huge soundstage for the bar scenes.

"How about *Friends of Dorothy?*" Stan chuckled, looking at the blank sign above the studio.

"*Dorothy's Friends?*" Rebel tilted his head to the side.

"Why does it have to scream gay?" Gareth frowned. "Why can't the sitcom have a normal name?"

"Hmm." Sebastian tapped his chin.

"*In and Out?*" Harley quipped.

"That's a burger joint." Achilles slapped Harley's butt playfully.

"*Adam and Adam.*" I blurted out.

"*The Wolf Den.*"

"*Bathsheba.*"

We all turned to look at Rebel. He grinned and wiggled his brows.

"How about *Route Sixty-Six?*" Axel piped up.

"*Route Sixty-Nine,*" Grandpa offered.

We all looked over at Grandpa, who had a shit-eating grin on his face.

"What?" He unconvincingly feigned innocence.

"Nothing," we all said in unison.

I glanced over at Sebastian, who seemed deep in thought. "Hey, Sebastian, have you found any other actors willing to play a gay man in this sitcom?"

"Where do you want me to start? Those who take the craft seriously couldn't care less what the role is as long as the story is great. I've got them coming out of the woodwork for this sitcom. Some of them have worked with Sal in the past — secondary characters, mind you, but they all love his work."

"That's awesome!" I said.

"Well, whoever I test with has to pass by Ransom as well." Sal put an arm around me.

"I trust you, Sal." I nudged his ear with my nose.

"I plan to watch it whatever night it's on." Harley grinned at us. "I think it's awesome. I don't think there is a show out there on the major networks which revolves around gay characters, especially since that other sitcom went off the air."

"We're going to shake things up." Sebastian nodded.

"I, for one, can't wait." I squeezed Sal tightly.

"Well, let's get a move on, lots of work to do today." Rebel began walking toward the building.

"I'm going to take Grandpa over to the nursing home." Stan took Grandpa's hand. "Then I'll be back."

"I can help. I can lay some wood." Grandpa grinned.

"Yeah, yeah, go on," Rebel laughed. "I'll be by to pick you up around six."

I stood with Sal as Stan maneuvered Grandpa into the car. Stan waved at us and I noticed Sal's face.

"What is it?" I asked.

"He looks so familiar. I can't quite figure it out."

"You too?" I said in surprise. "I've been wracking my brain trying to figure out who he reminds me of."

"I'm going to get Paul," Buster announced.

"Are you sure?" I asked.

"He wants to come help. It'll be good for him to get out of his room and do something constructive." Buster nodded.

"All right," I acquiesced.

"Well? Come on!" Axel glared at us.

Sal ran toward the building and I walked side by side with Gareth.

"So, you're going to take Sal to see Dad?" he asked.

"Yes, tomorrow. How do you think he'll react?"

"I think he'll be thrilled." Gareth took my hand.

By the end of the day, I was exhausted. Working with my hands was very therapeutic, however. I'd just gotten out of the shower and was sitting on the living room floor absently stringing the guitar when Sal walked in fresh from his own shower. He sat down next to me and rested his head on my shoulder.

"I forgot you play," he said.

"Well, I learned how to play before Gareth did. All of us pretty much know how to play all of the instruments. Of course, some of us are better at some than others."

"Jinx and the drums." Sal chuckled.

"Yeah. I can play enough to get by, but I'm really not very coordinated." I placed the guitar off to the side and turned to face him. He was nervously biting at his lower lip and I brushed my thumb against it. "What is it?"

Sal's eyes met mine and he tried to smile. "I know we've made love already, but can we wait until my next doctor's appointment to do it again?"

"Sal," I warned.

"I promise, I just need reassurance."

I took his face in my hands and kissed him lightly. "Fine, but don't try to pull away from me. I'm not with you for sex, Sal. You know that."

"I do," he nodded. "I just need to know I'm not putting you at risk."

"Do we need to see the doc again and have him walk you through the percentages?"

"Maybe?" Sal grinned.

"Whatever you want, Sal. I'm here, and I'm not leaving."

We stayed there, just staring into the fireplace. We didn't even need to speak; we were so at ease with each other. I'd told Sal a million times I couldn't care less if we ever had sex again — but he wasn't going to avoid it because he was scared. I knew what I'd signed up for and I was ready to move ahead with him. A slight snore met my ears and I glanced down to find him asleep. I grinned and pulled one of my throw blankets down, covering us both up.

"Ransom?" Sal mumbled, half asleep.

"Shh, just go back to sleep. You're okay." He was out again seconds later and I stared into the face of the man I loved. I gently traced his lips and touched them with my own lightly.

"It's all going to work out just fine. I promise."

We were on the road in the morning to Tucson and to the prison. I don't know why, but I felt as if my dad needed to meet Sal. He'd already accepted one gay son; I was hoping he'd be cool with a bisexual one. The thought made me laugh and Sal shot me a look from the passenger seat.

"Just thinking," I explained. "When Gareth came out, my dad didn't have any issue with it. Gareth and Axel took a trip to the prison because Axel wanted to be sure it wasn't my dad sending the threatening letters to Gareth. He was more concerned about the death threats than Gareth's sexuality."

"He sounds like a good man," Sal said.

"He didn't used to be. The drugs and alcohol and his condition made him an asshole. He's clean and sober now and on his meds. The last time I came down to see him, he looked really good."

"Well, I look forward to meeting him. What's his name?"

"Padriac, and yes, he expects you to call him that."

"That's SO Irish." Sal chuckled.

"Yeah, well, after the visit, I'm taking you out to the best sandwich place you've ever been to."

"Is that right?" Sal cocked a brow.

"Oh yeah."

I pulled into the parking lot and Sal got out, shielding his eyes from the sun. It was maybe seventy down in Tucson, but it felt hot compared to Flagstaff's temperatures. We walked in and I stopped in at the desk and signed in. Sal was looking around as the door buzzed and we were led into a room. My hands were sweating as we waited for my father to come out. Sal took my hands and gave me a reassuring grin. The door buzzed and my father strolled into the room. His eyes met mine and then he noticed Sal. His eyes went wide and he hurried over.

"Sal Falco!" he boomed.

A guard leapt in front of my father and he stepped back quickly, keeping his hands in front of him.

"Lord! I wasn't going to attack him! He's a flippin' movie star!"

"Mr. O'Donovan." Sal stood, extending a hand.

"No touching," the guard growled.

"You always bend the rules for me," I argued. I got a half-grin and a nod from the guard and I stood as well, hugging my father. "Hey, Dad."

"Frankenstein over there told me you were dating a movie star. He got me all the magazines with you and Sal on the cover." My dad motioned to the guard. He got raised brows from the man and grinned. "Okay, *Nash*."

"Nash, eh?" I smiled at the behemoth of a guard.

"Your guys should hire him on!" my dad exclaimed. "He's former military."

"Padriac, visit with your son." Nash cocked a brow.

"Well?" My father sat down, giddy it seemed. "So? Is it true? You two an item?"

I took Sal's hand. "Will you be okay with it?"

"Did Gareth go straight?" my father asked.

"Well, no."

"Then why would I care?"

"I like him," Sal said.

"He's moving to Flagstaff, Dad."

"Really?"

"Yes, really." Sal leaned forward in the chair, locking eyes with my father. "I love your son."

"Well, hell." My father grinned widely. "That's all a parent wants for their children, to be happy and loved. I look forward to seeing you together, maybe even married."

228

"One thing at a time, Dad," I chuckled.

We spent another half hour with him before leaving and heading back to Flagstaff. I stopped at my favorite sandwich shop and Sal got out of the car, looking at the sign.

"What is an eegee?" he asked.

"You've been missing out." I took his hand.

It seemed we'd caught the lunch rush and every person in line turned around as we walked in. A scream erupted from somewhere and then we had a crowd standing around us. Sal just laughed as people shoved whatever they could at him for a signature. I glanced up to see Hammer in the back of the store, keeping an eye out. I hadn't even realized he was there. He nodded and I smiled. After signing autographs, we finally got our food and sat in the back. Most of the people left us alone, but one small girl walked over to us shyly.

"Mr. Falco?" she said softly.

"Yes?"

"Could you sign my squid?"

"Of course I can. Would you like a picture too?"

She nodded and Sal glanced up to find her parents watching us. He waved them over and sat the little girl in his lap. After taking a few pictures, he signed her stuffed squid and placed a kiss on her cheek. She squealed and ran off. I couldn't stop smiling at him and he caught my eye.

"What?" he said.

"You are unbelievable, you know that?"

"Why? Because I signed a squid and took a picture?"

"No, because even though we were here for lunch and most celebrities would be pissed off to be interrupted, you signed at least fifty autographs, and took tons of pictures with all these people."

"So did you," Sal pointed out. "I'm just plain ol' Sal, remember?"

I took his hand and squeezed it. I knew we weren't out of the shit yet. Sal had come out and admitted he had HIV, and so far, we hadn't gotten too much bad press, but it would come. It always did. They wouldn't care what kind of man Sal was; they just wanted to get dirt on him.

"What's wrong?" Sal asked.

"I just know at some point the backlash is going to come."

"And we'll deal with it, Ransom. I knew what I was in for. It's worth it to be out with you here, or anywhere for that matter. I don't want to hide my feelings for you." Sal looked down at his food. "What did I order?"

"Just eat it. It's got provolone and three kinds of Italian meat on it. You'll love it, and don't forget to try the frozen drink."

Sal took my hand and kissed it. "Thank you."

"For what?"

"For being you."

We finished up lunch and signed more autographs on our way out. Sal waved and we got back in the car. I drove out to A Mountain, mainly because I wanted Sal to see the view of the city. I spent a lot of time in Tucson once I got older. When we started making up our tour schedule, we started spending at least a week in town before we even played.

Once we got to the top, I took Sal by the hand and we climbed the rest of the way up to the big 'A.' I stood behind Sal as we looked out over the city. The sun was beginning to set, painting lavender, red, and orange across the sky.

"Wow. No wonder you love it here."

"You will too, I promise."

"I already do."

Sal turned into my arms and I kissed him. If anyone was watching, it looked like an epic romantic movie — the wind blowing, the sky and its colors and the gorgeous man in my arms.

"Ready to go home?" I asked.

"Yes." Sal touched my cheek. "Home is with you."

Chapter 21

Things got hectic over the next two months. Sebastian and Sal were busy at the studio and we were still banging out tracks for the new album. By the time I got home, Sal was either still at the studio or passed out. We'd gone to see the doctor at his three-month checkup and his viral load was undetectable and his T-cell count was still high, but he was pulling away when we got intimate. I had been warned it could happen, but I thought Sal and I had gotten to a place where he could talk to me about how he was feeling.

We were taking all the precautions and I was still testing negative. We'd kissed, fondled, and gotten each other off, but Sal would always back off when we got *too* close. It was Saturday and the sun was out. Snow capped the mountains and the air was chilly. I wanted to spend my Saturday with Sal in bed, but he was already up and in the shower getting ready to leave for the studio. His phone dinged somewhere and I glanced around for it. I finally found it on the dresser and noticed Sebastian calling.

"Hey, Sebastian, he's in the shower."

"Tell him we're taking the day off. I'm dealing with my boys today."

I laughed at Sebastian referring to London Boys, his band he created as boys. Granted, they were all under the age of thirty, but Sebastian wasn't sixty. He was the same age as Sal and me.

"Your boys, eh?"

"Yes, my boys. They're tired and they need some fun time."

"Well, have fun with that. I'll let Sal know."

"And Ransom?"

"Yes?"

"Don't let him push you away. I know he's been working long hours to avoid being intimate."

"Yeah, I figured it out on my own, Sebastian, but thanks."

"Oooh, snarky! I love it. Bye, now!"

I laughed and hung up. Sal walked out of the bathroom, rubbing a towel over his wet hair. He looked mouth-watering wet.

"Hey." Sal grinned.

"Sebastian called. No work for you today."

"But I thought he wanted —"

"Stop it, Sal." I pointed at him. "You're not going to avoid me."

"What do you mean?"

"Don't play stupid, either. I know you've been pulling away from me and I'm done trying to handle this delicately. We're in this together and you need to stop thinking the way you're thinking!"

"How am I thinking?"

"That you're dirty somehow, and you're not! The people who have refused to work with you are narrow-minded idiots and have obviously never attended an HIV support group or even looked up what it means to have HIV." I walked over to him and took his face in my hands. "There is nothing wrong with you. Do you understand? You are a wonderful human being and I'm so lucky to have you in my life."

"I'm still... I don't know." Sal sighed in exasperation. "I'm not doing it on purpose."

I stared at the muscular chest in front of me, watching in fascination as water droplets trickled down his chest. I placed a hand over Sal's heart and closed my eyes, feeling his heart beating beneath my palm.

"Ransom —"

"Shhh."

My hand moved slowly downward. Sal's chest had a

slight dusting of soft hair and I followed it all the way down to the towel around his hips. I flicked the towel off and Sal gasped slightly. I cupped his cheek, our eyes locking as I began to stroke him slowly. His mouth opened, his lids dropped and I licked my lips as I watched his face. I cupped his nuts in my palm and slowly sank to my knees in front of him. His erection stood proud and I licked up the side, my hand mimicking my tongue. Sal's body shook as I laved around the rim of his cock, flicking all his sensitive spots. I moved back a bit and looked up at him.

"I want you to make me come."

"Oh, Ransom... I'm not —"

"Your fingers, Sal. Make me come with your fingers."

He sighed in relief and I walked over to the bed, lying down on my back, waiting for him. He crawled up on the bed and removed the lube from the drawer. He slicked two fingers and I cocked a brow.

"One at a time, I promise." He grinned slightly.

I nodded and let my legs fall off to the side, opening myself up to him. He settled between my open legs and leaned over me, brushing his lips against mine as he massaged around my hole first. I'd never had anything up my ass, but I trusted Sal would take good care of me. Sal slipped a finger inside me and I immediately tried to push it out. My stomach clenched and a burn shot up my spine and into my shoulders.

"Relax," Sal said against my lips. "Just let me in."

"Trying," I choked out.

"I promise, when I find your spot, you'll forget about all the pain you feel right now."

I wanted to believe him. I really did. But when he added a second finger I almost jumped off the bed. Sal kept kissing me, keeping me occupied while his fingers stretched me out. He pushed up and a cry left my lips.

"There it is." Sal smiled against my mouth.

"Fuck!" I spluttered.

"Now I've got you."

Holy hell and fuck me running it felt so fucking *good!* Sal repeatedly nailed my spot. My dick was so hard I could have hammered nails with it. Sal began jacking me off with his free hand while he fingered my ass. I was seeing spots. My breathing became erratic and my gut had reached a boiling point. Sal's mouth covered my cock, the suction began and the fire erupted in my balls shooting out my dick. I think I screamed. Sal was sucking me down, a groan left him, and then I felt his release hit my thigh. The guy had gotten off just listening to me. How fucking hot was that? Sal pulled off my dick, licking his lips, and he smiled down at me.

"How was that?"

"Holy shit!" I yanked him down into my arms and he

tried to get out of my grasp.

"I gotta clean up."

"No, I'm not going to get HIV from your cum drying on my leg. Stop it, Sal." I pulled him close and kissed his forehead. "How many times do I have to say we're in this together?"

"I know, I'm sorry. It's just going to take a bit."

"Why don't we go out today? It's still early."

"Sure. Where?"

"I don't know, maybe up to Snow Bowl? Wanna ski?"

"I don't ski. I fall."

"Well, it seems most of us can't ski," I chortled. "Jinx doesn't, either. Just makes igloos and snowmen."

"Why don't we go see Paul? He could probably use the company."

I sat up, holding Sal close to me. "I love that you think of him the way you do."

"I can't even imagine what he went through, but he's very lucky to have you and the guys watching out for him."

My phone pinged and I grabbed it off the table. Gareth was texting me. I glanced up at Sal. "How about a trip to Gareth's tree house?"

"Sounds like a good idea."

"I guess all the guys are going, even Paul."

"Well, let's head out then."

I got up and headed to the bathroom to wash. Sal was already in the kitchen by the time I got out. I headed to the back room and stopped at the entrance to the guest room. My mother's dresser sat in the corner; the sun's rays filtering through the window gave it an ethereal glow. I stepped into the room and walked over to it. I closed my eyes as I ran a hand over the top of the wood. I could almost hear her laugh.

"Hey."

I turned to find Sal behind me, fidgeting and unsure if he should have interrupted me. I motioned him to come over and then opened the middle drawer.

I lifted out a small box and cracked it open slightly.

"What is it?" Sal asked.

I opened it more and stared at two locks of hair along with footprints in plaster. It was mine and Gareth's hair, along with our foot and handprints. There were also pictures of her holding us, and what looked like our hospital bands.

"She loved you both so much," Sal said, picking up the tiny hospital bands.

"I miss her, you know? Some days more than others. She was always there for us when we got a bump or a bruise. She always said being a real man meant you could show your weaknesses."

"And what a man you turned out to be, Ransom Fox."

238

I glanced over at Sal and smiled. I placed the box back in the drawer, shut it, and took him in my arms.

"Thank you for being here."

"Any time, Ransom."

We headed out to Gareth's with the windows down even though it was in the low thirties outside. The fresh mountain air felt and smelled wonderful.

"I can't believe he has a tree house," Sal mused.

"Gareth has always wanted one, so he had one built."

We pulled up to the bridge and parked next to the side with all the other cars. Sal stepped carefully on to the bridge and looked over the side.

"Don't look down." I laughed, grabbing his hand. We crossed without incident and I knocked once before opening the door and walking in. Gareth was on the couch with Axel and the rest of the guys were spread out in the living room.

"Hey, Ransom!" Gareth jumped up and came over to Sal, hugging me before turning his attention to Sal and grabbing him as well. "Thanks for coming!"

"What are you guys up to?"

"Just hanging out, but Evander came to visit, so I figured we'd all get together."

"Evander is one of the other London Boys, right?" Sal asked.

"Yep. He and Jayden are pretty close." Gareth walked backward, taking our hands and pulling us along.

Sandrine Gasq-Dion

"And aren't they supposed to be with Sebastian?" I asked suspiciously, eyebrows raised.

Ransom grinned. "Only long enough to convince you to spend your day with me."

"Hey, Sal!" Rebel waved him over.

"I'm good," I assured Sal. "Go hang out."

I followed Gareth out to the deck and we both leaned against the rail, looking out over Sedona below. Gareth took my hand and squeezed it.

"Have I told you how happy I am for you?"

"Yes, you did." I took in the beauty before me and let out a slow breath.

"You finally got your happily ever after."

I glanced over my shoulder to see Sal laughing with the guys. Our eyes met and I grinned.

"True love doesn't have a happy ending, Gareth. True love never ends." I looked back at Gareth to see a huge grin on his face. "Oh God, that was cheesy, huh?"

"It's so good to see you cheesy, Ransom. I love that you finally found the one person who clicks."

"You're just glad I'm going to let up on you now."

"That's an advantage." Gareth hugged me. "I want you to have a life of your own. Like I said before, I'm good now. I have love in my life and I'm so much stronger because of it. You don't have to worry about me anymore — or Harley, for that matter."

240

"I know. I'm so glad Achilles came into his life." The sliding door opened and Harley, Jinx, Rebel, and Paul walked out to join us. We all leaned against the deck railing and stared out at the red rock stretched out for miles.

"Sal was just telling us they handed out tickets to the first live taping of the show to the kids at the LGBT youth center," Harley said.

"I'm looking forward to it." I nodded. "It's going to be so cool to fly all those kids out and put them up for a few days. Sal wants to be a lot more involved now."

"Where's Stan?" Paul asked.

"With my gramps. They're interviewing new at-home care nurses."

"Didn't you just hire one?" I asked.

"He did." Jinx laughed. "But Gramps offended her somehow."

"I swear he does it on purpose, Rebel. I don't think he wants you to leave him," Harley pointed out.

"I'm trying to take care of him, and Stan does a lot, probably too much. I feel like I'm relying on him more and more." Rebel sighed.

"I think if Stan had an issue with it, he'd say so, Rebel. Stan truly cares for Gramps and he gets to spend time with you as well. I'm sure that's a plus." Paul grinned.

"Meaning?" Rebel lifted a brow.

"Oh, come on!" I balked. "Don't stand there and tell

us you've never noticed Stan mooning over you!"

"He looks at me, so what? Doesn't mean anything." Rebel shook his head.

"Okay, enough about Stan and his love for all things Rebel," Jinx cut in. "We have a few things to take care of over the next few weeks. I'd like to spend some time with my man."

"Me too," I said, staring at Sal through the window.

"So? Let's get a move on." Jinx walked back into the house.

I stayed on the deck, watching Sal with the bodyguards. He seemed so at ease with them. Our eyes met and he winked.

"Ransom?" Gareth pulled me out of my daze.

"Yep?"

"Ready?"

Yeah. I was ready for anything.

EPILOGUE

I took Sal into town the following week. I could tell depression was creeping in. Whether it was his HIV diagnosis or the fact that quite a few people in Hollywood had turned their backs on him, I wasn't sure, but I wasn't going to let him wallow. I had formulated a plan and was putting it into action. I pulled up in front of the hospital and Sal turned in the seat to look at me.

"You didn't tell me we were coming to see Paul."

"I didn't?" I grinned, getting out of the car. I came around the front and Sal locked his side. I held up my keys and hit the button to unlock the doors. Sal narrowed his eyes and I yanked open the door.

"Get out, ya big baby."

Sal huffed, but got out of the car. I took his hand as we walked up to the hospital doors. I stopped at the handle to the door and eyed him.

"Be good."

"Pfft." Sal blew his hair out of his eyes.

I opened the door and stepped in. It was dark, and as soon as Sal walked in, the lights went up and everyone yelled 'surprise!' Sal looked shocked and then a smile formed on his lips. He turned to me and lifted his brows.

"What is all this?" he asked.

"This, my friend, is your intervention."

Sal's mouth dropped open. "Jasper?"

"Yep." Jasper grinned and stepped forward, taking Sal's hand. "When Ransom called and said you were down in the dumps, I had to come out here and see for myself. Guys like us have to stick together, Sal."

"Guys like us?" Sal said in confusion.

"HIV, Sal. We both have it," Jasper explained.

"Wait... what? But you're..."

"Straight? Yep, I sure am. Doesn't mean I can't get it, Sal. I told you I was reckless in my youth."

"How long have you... you know, known?"

"Almost six years, buddy. I know what you're going through, so if you ever need me, I'm just a phone call away."

I smiled as everyone came forward to hug Sal. I'd even flown in Fergus and he grabbed Sal and crushed him in a hug. Sal glanced over his shoulder as Fergus led him away and I winked at him. Gareth came to my side and held

---

my hand.

"He needed this," he said.

"Yes, he did. He needs to know there is nothing wrong with him. He deserves to be loved, touched, and kissed. There are going to be hard times ahead and I plan to stick by him whether he likes it or not."

"How did you get Jasper Jamison out here?"

"He called me. He explained how he felt when he was first diagnosed, and said if he could be any help just to call him. Well, I did."

Jinx, Harley, Rebel, and Paul all came to stand with me and Gareth and we watched as everyone hugged Sal, giving him encouragement. I'd brought the HIV support group out to take part in my little plan and they were more than willing to sit down and talk with Sal. He'd been fighting me on attending, so this was my way of getting him to go.

"He's going to be just fine, Ransom," Paul said. "We'll all be here to whip him if he fucks up."

I took a look at the guys by my side. Through thick and thin we'd always been together.

We always would be, and now Sal was part of the family.

"Yeah. Yeah, we will."

Sandrine Gasq-Dion

LINK

Don't wait. If you think you may have HIV, get tested.
http://www.thestdproject.com/std-resources/hiv-support-groups-by-location/

There are people who care.
http://www.tihan.org

Sandrine Gasq-Dion

OTHER WORKS:

Start the ride from the beginning with: A Marked Man; Alaska with Love; By the light of the Moon; Half Moon Rising; Best Laid Plans; For the Love of Caden; The General's Lover; Russian Prey; An Ignited Passion; Reflash; The Red Zone; Irish Wishes; Pleading the Fifth ; Betrayed; Summer of Awakenings; Into the Lyons Den; The Nik of Time and The Littlest Assassin-Shifters; Lessons Learned; Broken Bonds and Forbidden; Dirty Ross; Savage Love; Locke and Key, and Tricked, Bewildered and Bitten

The 12 Olympians: Justice for Skylar; At Year's End; Lux Ex Tenebris; Strange Addiction; Ryde the Lightning, Wraith and The Hard Rhoade

From Wilde City Publishing: A Betting Man ; A Marrying Man and A Fighting Man; A Working Man and A Healing Man; A Selfless Man and An Honorable Man

The Medicine and The Mob; An Eye For an Eye; The Harder they Fall; What Goes Around and

248

Karma; Reflections; Open Doors; Beginnings; Making the Rules and V Is for Vicious; Russian Roulette
The Rock Series: FRET; Jinxed and Harley's Achilles

And, Second Time Around and Gabriel's Fall
Join me on my Facebook pages!
https://www.facebook.com/pages/Official-Sandrine-Gasq-Dion/137320826386776?ref=hl
@Sandrine_GasqD

Need a family tree? Here's the link to it!

https://sites.google.com/site/assassinshiftertree/

76554315R00140

Made in the USA
San Bernardino, CA
13 May 2018